# VALLEY JUSTICE

•••••

*"Clear out, Bax," Jim said evenly. "It's all over. You've nothing to gain by a shoot-out."*

*LeFarge laughed viciously. "I knowed you was yellow! You may be handy with your fists, but I'm tellin' you you're finished, Reno."*

*Reno was aware that LeFarge would not back down, and a great regret swept over him. He said mildly, "I wish you'd left, Bax."*

*"You knew I wouldn't, didn't you? I'd never walk away from a fight. When I leave here, you won't be goin' anywhere."*

*Reno had his entire attention fixed on LeFarge, staring into his hate-filled eyes. His own nerves were straining, and at the first sign of a movement of LeFarge's right hand, he would go for his own gun.*

GILBERT MORRIS

# VALLEY JUSTICE

Tyndale House Publishers, Inc.
Wheaton, Illinois

**Library of Congress Cataloging-in-Publication Data**

Morris, Gilbert.
  Valley justice / Gilbert Morris.
    p.   cm. — (Reno western saga ; 5)
   ISBN 0-8423-7756-5
   I. Title.  II. Series: Morris, Gilbert.   Reno western saga ; 5.
PS3563.08742V29   1995
813′.54—dc20                                94-26129

Printed in the United States of America

99  98  97  96  95
7   6   5   4   3   2   1

*To Ken Petersen*

*I've always been jealous of guys who are better looking than I am—or have more charm or better physiques. But since none of these apply to you, Ken, I'm happy to announce that our friendship is on firm ground.*

*Thanks for all the support you've given Johnnie and me for so long. You are the nonpareil of editors, and we are grateful for you!*

# ONE
## A Voice from the Past

*I wonder if there was ever a pretty mining camp.*

Jim Reno let the thought run through his mind as he entered Virginia City. But as he swung off his tired horse and tied him to the hitching post, he decided there probably wasn't. Turning to his right, he made his way down the main street marked out by tents and brush wickiups and a few board houses. Like all boom camps, this one had been hurriedly thrown together with cheap lumber, canvas, and logs. Fully three-quarters of the camp was made up of saloons and dance halls; the rest of it consisted of stores, miners' supply houses, livery barns, and restaurants. Reno traced his way down the street, speaking to the roughly dressed men he passed.

A violent southwest wind rolled ragged black clouds low over the town, and the flatly swollen drops of an intemperate rain formed a slanting silver screen all around him, dimpling the street's watery mud and dancing a crystal dance on the glistening rooftops. The plank walkways across the street intersections were half afloat and sagged beneath his weight as he used them. At two o'clock on such a dark day the kerosene lights were sparkling through drenched panes, and the smell of saloons when he moved by them was a rich, warm blend of tobacco, whiskey, and wet leather.

Reno approached a store with "Creighton's General Store" painted on a large board outside. He entered the unpainted wooden building that was nestled between a blacksmith's shop and a saloon. The interior was dimly lit by three lanterns, which cast their feeble glow over jumbled wares. The floor was crowded with barrels, saddles, harnesses, boxes, and crates, while on the walls canned goods, clothing, cooking utensils, and a hundred other items filled the rough shelves.

"Hello, Jim. Haven't seen you for a while." A tall, stately man with white hair and a Vandyke beard moved out of the back room to stand before Jim Reno. Len Creighton was one of the more cultured citizens of Virginia City; he wore a suit with a black string tie, even as he did his clerking. "Where've you been hiding?" he asked genially.

"Trying to get rich, I guess," Reno said, smiling wryly.

"Well," Creighton answered, a humorous light in his eyes, "I hope you're doing better at it than some I've seen here at Alder Gulch." He studied Reno quietly and, as always, was impressed by the man. Reno stood no more than five feet, ten inches, and weighed about 175 pounds, but Creighton did not miss the smooth-flowing muscles of the upper body of Jim Reno. Reno's hair lay thick and black and ragged against his temples, and his eyes were sleepy under jet brows. He had a small scar over his right temple and did not look his age, which was twenty-seven. There was a sleepy look about him, but his enemies had learned how quickly the temper that lay buried under the calm exterior could flare.

Creighton snapped his fingers. "Oh—got a letter for you, Jim. Just a minute." He turned, walked behind the counter, pulled an envelope out of a box nailed to the wall, brought it back, and handed it to the waiting Reno. "Thought you'd be in before this," he apologized. "Thought once about sending it out, but—"

"That's OK, Len," Reno said. He glanced at the envelope, then looked up at the storekeeper with an odd expression in his dark eyes. "Comes as kind of a shock, getting a letter from someone I haven't thought of for a spell." He reached into his pocket and gave Creighton a rather grubby paper, saying, "Throw this in a box for me, will you, Len?"

"Sure." The storekeeper nodded and turned to the task of filling the order.

Reno moved away from the counter, leaned against a post, and let the pale lantern light fall on the letter. He studied it for a moment, thoughts running through his mind, then he carefully opened the envelope, removed a single sheet of paper, and unfolded it. He stood there running his eyes over the brief letter and grew very still. When he had finished, he slowly folded the letter, put it back in the envelope, and stuck it in his shirt pocket. A thoughtful look touched his eyes, and he remained where he was, his body still but his mind running quickly. He was a man who loved action but had learned the value of rest and reflection in the intermediate times.

He stood there until Creighton called out, "Got your order, Jim." Then he moved over, asked the total, and paid the owner out of a sack of gold dust he kept in his coat pocket. Creighton weighed it carefully on a scale, tightened the poke, handed it back, and said, "Why don't you bring Lee and Easy in and the three of you throw a big bust? It's not natural for men to work as hard as you three have."

"Might just do that. Easy's chompin' at the bit." Reno nodded at the groceries and said, "I'll be back. Put those away somewhere for a while if you will, Len. I got a visit to make."

"Give the widow Warren my regards," Creighton said, and his mouth turned upward in a smile. He considered Reno for a moment, then shook his head. "A lot of men in this camp feel pretty hard, Jim. You've got the only good-looking woman in the camp for your lady friend."

Reno didn't answer directly. "I'll be back for the grub, Len." Then he turned and left the store rapidly. The rain was coming down harder now, making a brown, slick river of mud over the streets. He pulled his hat down firmly on his head, climbed on his horse, and rode down the street, his shoulders hunched.

A four-horse dray came up the street at that moment, the great wheels plunging half to the hub. The teamster cursed vigorously, and Reno smiled slightly as he passed by. Off to his left an old man with a set of muttonchop whiskers plastered to his jowls tentatively ventured off the plank sidewalk, mud flowing around his unsteady feet.

Leaving the main street behind, Reno turned off to another muddy road that wound crookedly past Virginia City's other blacksmith shop and eventually out of town. Pulling up to one of the log huts that had been built close to a lawn of alders, he stepped off his horse, tied him, then went to the door and knocked. It opened almost at once, and Reno took off his hat, saying, "Wet out here, Rachel."

Rachel Warren smiled at Reno as she reached out and felt his sleeve. "You're soaked to the skin!" she exclaimed. "Come inside and dry out." She pulled him inside, yanked off his coat, shoved him into a chair, and began bustling about the wood stove, brewing coffee in a heavy pot. She was twenty-six, this woman with dark, almost purple eyes, and a sleek cap of brown hair. Her husband had died at Belle Isle, a Confederate prison camp, and when she had first met Jim Reno, she had hated him as she hated all Southerners. But as time had passed, she had learned to set aside her prejudice—starting with this one Southerner.

Finally the coffee was done. She poured two cups and sat down, and the two of them began drinking. "I thought you'd left the country," Rachel said with a smile. She had a good smile, warm and cheerful. Impulsively she reached over and put her hand on his as it rested on the table. "Haven't you men pulled enough dust out to take a little break?"

"I guess we're all pretty tired of grubbing in the dirt." Reno shrugged. He sipped his coffee and sat looking at her thoughtfully. He remembered how her eyes had held nothing but disdain for him when they had first met. But now they were warm, and he wondered if this would be the woman for him. He had had hopes, for his life had been lonely and he never had a proper home. The war had taken a big chunk out of his life, and since Appomattox he had wandered over the West, mostly alone.

But now he and his two partners had taken enough money out of the ground to do something with, to start a life somewhere. He had no desire at all to be a miner all his life. It was a rough, crude, boring job—taking the best out of a man and leaving very little else.

He sipped the coffee and then said, "I got something to tell you." Reaching into his pocket, he pulled out the letter and held it up before Rachel. "This was waiting for me when I went into Creighton's," he said. "I figured you better know about it right away."

Rachel's eyes focused on the name and address on the envelope. "Martin Reynolds," she murmured and then turned her eyes back up to Jim. "Who is he?"

"Just about the best friend I ever had," Reno said quietly. "He was my commander during the war, but I guess he was more than that." The rain beat on the shake roof, making a groaning noise, and he sat there listening to it for a moment and looking through the single window as the water fell in a steady sheet. Memories flooded him; he thought of the war and of the man who had written this letter. "I never knew a man like Martin Reynolds, Rachel. I was a pretty wild young buck when I signed up, and if it hadn't been for Major Reynolds, I never would have made it through the war. He was my company commander, and he stopped me from committing suicide more than once." A grin touched his long lips, and he shook his head at the old memories coming to him. "I thought I had to finish the war off all by myself," he said, "and I would've tried it, I guess, if Major Reynolds hadn't been there to stop me from charging the whole Union army."

The mention of the war disturbed Rachel as it always did. She was a woman of strong emotions, and she had loved her husband. It had taken every bit of strength she had to put away the thoughts of his terrible death in the Confederate prison. At times she thought she had completely forgotten— but then, in the night, in the silence, the memories of how much she had loved him and how the war had torn him from her would come flooding back. Nervously she smoothed her hair and asked, "What does Major Reynolds say, Jim?"

Reno hesitated, not knowing exactly how to put the thing. "Let me read this letter to you," he said and quickly raised the letter and began to read. It said:

Dear Jim,

I have no idea if this letter will ever reach you or not. I lost track of you some time ago, and your last letter had no return address. That was over a year ago, and since then I haven't heard. I'd hoped you would write, and I'd hoped you'd be coming East so we could see each other once again. I don't miss a great many things about the war, but there are a few things I do miss. Of course, one is getting to see the men of the company.

I hate to ask favors. I always did. And I know that you do, too, Jim. But I'm in considerable difficulty, and I can't think of anyone who can help unless it would be you. I thought a bullet would get me in the war, and it didn't, but something's got me now. The doctor says I'm in bad shape, and what he really means is I'm not going to get off this bed. I got sick about six months ago and went downhill fast, and now, like an old dog, I sense death coming on. Oh, I'm not complaining, Jim, I've had a good life, but there are things I need to do for my family that are out of my control, and I need a man to help.

Last week Charlie Kimble came to see me. You remember Charlie, he was the lieutenant of I Company. He said a friend of his ran into you in the Alder Gulch mining camp. He didn't have any address, and he wasn't sure you were still there. But I'm taking a chance that you will be and an even bigger chance that you'll be willing to drop what you're doing and come and give me a hand.

If it's impossible, Jim, for you to come, I don't want you to worry about it. I know you'd do anything you could, but sometimes we just can't help ourselves. So if circumstances are such that you can't come, don't let it grieve you. If that is the case, I'll just take this opportunity to say good-bye. You were a fine soldier, Jim, maybe the best I ever knew, and I treasure the times we had together. The cause was lost; but that thing that existed between old soldiers is never lost. Hoping to see you, but if not, God be with you and keep you all of your days.

Martin Reynolds

Reno glanced at Rachel. "When I read that it was like one time when I got hit in the stomach. Sort of paralyzed me. I couldn't move, couldn't hardly think." He got up and walked over to the window, his back tense, his head turned away from her. When he spoke his voice was low. "There never was a finer man than Martin Reynolds. Not that I've ever met."

Rachel did not speak for a moment, but when she did there was a peculiar quality in her voice that Reno had not heard for some time. "You're leaving here, aren't you, Jim? To go to him? Major Reynolds?"

"Why, I'll have to." Reno turned and walked back over and took his seat again, picked up his coffee, and sipped it without thinking. His mind was on the man so far away. "I'll have to go, Rachel. It's a call from a friend." He looked searchingly at her and said, "It's not something I can say no to, is it?"

"I don't know, Jim," Rachel said slowly. She held her hands tightly together and twisted them. He sat there quietly, waiting, and she looked down at her hands thoughtfully and then raised her eyes to him. "I . . . thought we were . . . had plans. I know," she said quickly, "that you never asked me, but I thought we would be married someday."

Reno said at once, "That may be, Rachel. I think a lot of

you. You're a fine woman." He hesitated, then leaned slightly toward her. "I'm just saying we'll have to wait a while."

Rachel got up and paced the floor, and then she began to speak very rapidly. She spoke of her life and how she'd had to wait so long to get married because of her father's illness, then how she'd waited while her husband had gone away to the war, never to return, and finally she turned to him, saying, "And now I'm ready to live, Jim, and you're asking me to wait again."

"Why, it won't be that long—"

"You don't know that," she said harshly. She stopped at the sound of her own voice and then took a deep breath. "I've got to tell you something. It's been on my mind a long time." She hesitated and dropped her eyes. After a moment she looked back up, saying, "You're a traveling man, Jim Reno. How many times have you told me about the places you've been and how you've liked it? But I thought that was over— that you'd stay here and we'd get married. But it can't be like that, can it? You're not the kind of man to put down roots."

Reno shifted uneasily and put his cup down. "Well, some of it wasn't my choice, Rachel," he said, making his defense quickly. "I didn't have much choice about going to the war, and afterwards it was pretty much a matter of just bummin' around trying to keep body and soul together. But when I get this chore done, I've got some money now—"

But Rachel was shaking her head. "No, that's not the way it will be, Jim. You're not a settled man. I saw it from the first but tried to ignore it, and I can't live from pillar to post. I'm going to find a man who wants to stay in one place all of his life. If that sounds selfish," she added with a shrug, "I guess it'll have to be. I hate to sound that way, but it's the truth."

Reno sat there and tried to argue, but he saw her mind

was made up. Finally she said firmly, "You go on to Chicago, Jim, and do what you have to do. You don't even know how long it will take and, of course, I couldn't ask you not to go help your friend. But put me out of your mind, and I'll put you out of mine." She hesitated, and he thought he saw a break in her resolution. Her eyes seemed to go tender—but quickly she blinked, and her lips tightened firmly. "It's better this way, I think. We're too different."

Reno stood up, picked up his hat, and turned it around in his hands. He knew little about women, but he knew one thing: This was a strong, firm woman, this Rachel Warren. She was not one whose mind could be easily changed, and he had gotten to know her well enough to know that her decision was firm. He said slowly, "I don't think it's altogether this trip, is it, Rachel? You've been thinking about this for quite a while."

Rachel nodded. "Yes, I have."

He took a deep breath, turned, and grabbed his coat. As he opened the door, he put his hat on and nodded to her. "I probably won't be seeing you for a while. This sounds pretty urgent to me. So I'll just say good-bye for now."

"Good-bye, Jim." She walked to the door and put her hand out. Reno took her hand in both of his, then leaned in and kissed her right cheek. When he stepped back, she nodded. "I wish you well. But put me out of your mind."

She stepped inside and shut the door. There was a finality in the sound that rang in Reno's mind. He got on his horse and rode away through the sheets of falling rain and did not look back at the cabin.

# Two
## A Cold Reception

Reno cinched the saddle of the tall bay tightly, lowered the stirrup, then turned and said to the boy waiting beside him, "I know you'd like to go, Lee, but I just don't know what I'm going to run into."

Lee Morgan could not hide the disappointment in his blue eyes. He brushed back the fair hair that fell over his forehead and put his hands on his hips. "I don't see why I can't come, Jim. It ain't no fun to stay here."

Reno slapped the boy on the back. "I know it's not. And as soon as I get this business settled, I think we'll sell out and get out of this place. I've had about enough grubbin' in the ground." He glanced over at the man lounging beside the shack and said, "How about you, Easy?"

Easy Jones, bandy-legged, wiry, and tough, grinned back at him. He had tow-colored hair and a huge plow of a nose. He was not over five feet, six inches, but he was tough as whanged leather. "I was ready to go the day after we got here," he said. "I don't wanna put no good moles outta work, and that's about all we been doin' that I can see. Why don't we all just bundle up and go with you?"

Reno shook his head regretfully. "I wish you could, but we're going to need a stake when we leave here—so you two are elected to do the hard work." He turned to leave, put his hand on Lee's shoulder, and studied the boy's face. At fourteen, Lee was on the verge of early manhood and stood as tall as Reno himself. Reno thought back to the time he had taken the boy in when he was a poor, scared orphan, bitter and mad at the world. *He's changed a lot since then,* Reno thought proudly. *He's going to be a fine man.* But he only said, "Look, I don't know what's coming up on this trip. Major Reynolds may be dead, for all I know. I may turn right around and come back. But it may turn out to be something bigger than that. So you two are going to have to mind the store while I'm gone, OK?" He squeezed the boy's shoulder and felt a strong wave of affection for him.

"OK, Jim," Lee sighed. "If that's the way it is, we'll do 'er. But don't make us wait too long, OK?"

Reno slapped the boy on the back, hard. "OK. You keep an eye on Easy, now, and don't let him get into trouble." He swung into the saddle, touched his spurs to the bay, and the horse wheeled around. As he sped out of the camp, he turned and waved, noting the disappointment on the faces of both of his friends. "See you soon!" he hollered and then turned away.

By late afternoon Reno arrived in the small town touched by the railroad. After he was told by the stationmaster that the train east wasn't due in until the next morning, Reno sold his horse and gear, rented a room, and got some sleep. When the train came the next day, Reno got on, carrying only one small satchel.

He found a seat and for the next four days endured the difficulties of 1872 railroad travel. When he finally heard the conductor say, "Chicago! All out for Chicago!" he thought, *This trip's made me more tired than any trail drive I ever made.* He stepped out of the murky and smoke-blackened train and caught a reflection of himself in the window. *I look like a coal miner who forgot to wash!* His face and hands were streaked with smoke and dust, and his clothing was wrinkled and smutty. His three nights on the railroad had not permitted him much cleaning up.

A hack driver who saw him lugging his valise out of the railroad shed said, "Hack, sir?" Reno hesitated, but the driver seized the satchel and put it in his battered vehicle. He was an old man with an Irish face. A fringe of white hair stood out under his tall hat. "Where do you want to go?"

Reno said, "Take me to a pretty nice hotel. But not too nice."

"Yes, sir. The charge will be a dollar, though."

"That'll be all right." A dollar didn't seem like much after the gold fields.

Jim leaned back and took in Chicago, or as much as he could see of it, as the hack moved along. What his eyes saw caught him by surprise. He had overheard people on the train talking about a fire in Chicago, but he had had no idea of the devastation. The city blocks were a tangle of cinders and blackened rubble. As the hack moved steadily north, a few newer buildings, obviously built since the inferno, jutted up out of the heaps of ash and crumbled walls. While Reno had seen destruction during the war, this struck him as more tragic, since so many women and children were the victims of this disaster.

The words of one man on the train—a Georgian, judging by his accent—echoed in Reno's mind, "Reckon this just 'bout makes up for what them Yanks did to Atlanta!"

It was Sunday morning, and church bells were ringing. They passed a large, handsome, newly built wooden church, and many groups of people were coming down the street on their way to the service. All the men wore tall silk hats and the long double-breasted frock coats known as Prince Alberts. Most of the women wore hoop skirts that Reno had heard about but never seen. Some of the bustles that he saw stood out twelve or fifteen or even eighteen inches behind their wearers. The skirts were long, so long that the hems collected dust and refuse from the ground. All the ladies wore over-dresses of colored silk. These outside garments were ornamented with embroidered flowers and other decorations.

The hackman pulled up suddenly before the entrance to a hotel. Reno got out and gave him a dollar with a fifty-cent tip, receiving a happy "Thank you, sir!" for it. He picked up his valise and carried it through an impressive doorway into a huge lobby. The floor was covered by a dark green carpet that was speckled here and there by brass cuspidors, or spittoons as they were more commonly called.

The hotel registration desk stood almost directly opposite the hotel entrance. Reno walked over, and the clerk, a young man who wore side-whiskers, gave him a professional smile and placed the register before him. Reno wrote his name and paused in reflection, finally writing down "Alder Gulch, Montana," and shoved the register back.

"Take room 407," the clerk said, handing him a key. "Hope you enjoy your visit."

Reno walked around, looking for the stairs. In front of him a door opened, and three people walked out of what seemed to be a very small room. Reno had heard of elevators but had never seen one. When he tentatively entered, an elderly man sitting on a stool asked him, "What floor?" After he replied, the man shut the doors and pushed a button. The elevator went up at a snail's pace, so slow it hardly seemed to be moving.

*I liked that. Wait till Lee and Easy hear I rode in an elevator,* Reno thought as he got off on the fourth floor. Down the hall he found room 407, in which there was a poster bed wide enough for three people. It had a bathroom equipped with a large bathtub made of zinc, its sides encased in wood. It had a washbasin also, surrounded by a wooden frame that reached down to the floor, concealing the plumbing.

Reno was tired after his trip. He undressed and got into the bathtub he'd filled with water, soaking the dirt and grime and soot away. He'd had a rough time sleeping on the train, so he fell asleep in the tub. When he awoke, he dried off and headed for the bedroom to get dressed. The big bed looked inviting, so he lay down and at once was asleep again.

He woke up sometime in the middle of the night, fear running over him when he didn't recognize his surroundings. Then it came back to him, and he smiled and went back to sleep.

He rose before dawn, shaved, and put on the fresh clothes he'd brought in his satchel: a pair of dark gray pants, a white shirt with full sleeves, and a string tie. He wore the short boots with high heels and the same black low-crowned hat that he'd left the mining camp wearing.

He sat around the room impatiently, and finally, when dawn came, he went down and had breakfast in the hotel restaurant. After a filling meal of eggs, bacon, and waffles with maple syrup, Reno went out and found a hack. "Do you know the way to Barton Street?" he asked.

"Sure. Get in."

Reno gave the driver the address and settled into the hack. Fifteen minutes later he got out on a street on the north side of Chicago, which was near the shore of Lake Michigan. As he rode, Reno noticed that the fire had spared this section of Chicago. "This is it," the hack driver said, waving toward a large brownstone house set well back from the road. "Fare's two dollars."

Reno gave him the money, knowing he was being over-charged, but he had no desire to argue; instead, Reno "forgot" to tip the man. Turning, he walked up the big cobblestone side-walk to the house and sounded the heavy brass knocker mounted on the large door. While he waited, he looked over the house. It was built of reddish brick, two stories high, and had a lawn and flower garden. One side of a wide driveway led up to a carriage house. The porch in front was so wide and sat so low that it kept the rooms on the lower floor well shaded. A large weather vane on the ridge of the roof shaped like a flying goose creaked noisily with every little gust of wind.

The door opened, and a diminutive maid with a pair of sharp black eyes looked up at him. "Yes, sir?" she inquired.

"I'd like to see Major Reynolds," Reno said.

"Oh, I'm sorry, Major Reynolds doesn't receive any visi-tors."

Reno hesitated, then asked, "Could I see Mrs. Reynolds, then?"

The maid stepped back, saying, "Come in. I'll tell Mrs. Reynolds you're here."

Reno removed his hat, followed her into a small room off the wide foyer, and waited as the maid disappeared. It was an expensive house, he realized. The furniture was of black walnut and mahogany, and gleamed by the light of the many lamps that burned in the room. *At least the major's not dead,* he thought. *She would've told me that.* He was glad that he had made it before his friend died.

"Yes? I'm Mrs. Reynolds."

Reno turned quickly to face the woman who had entered the room. She was a pretty woman with delicate features. She had auburn hair, brown eyes, and a rather small mouth. "My name's Jim Reno, Mrs. Reynolds. I was in your husband's company during the war."

Mrs. Reynolds stared at him, then said, "Perhaps you didn't know, but my husband is very ill. Too ill to see anyone."

"I think he might like to see me," Reno said. "I got a letter from him, asking me to come, and I've come a long way."

"Well, I'll have to ask him. You wait here, please."

Again Reno waited and wondered what sort of condition Major Reynolds was in. Finally the woman returned, looking displeased. "He wants to see you," she said, "but you mustn't stay long."

She turned and led the way down a wide hall to a room at the end. She opened the door, and Jim murmured, "Thank you, Mrs. Reynolds," and entered the room. He heard the door close behind him and looked across to see a man sitting up in bed. Shock ran through him, for he remembered Martin Reynolds as a big man with lively brown eyes and thick hair. What he saw was a skeleton, really—a sick man with thin hair turned completely gray, with cheeks sunken in, and eyes sunken also. He advanced quickly, saying, "Major Reynolds, I'm glad to see you."

The hand that Reynolds held out was nothing but skin covering bone, and there was no strength in his grasp. A light gleamed in his dull eyes, and his sunken lips turned up in a smile. "Hello, Jim. I'm glad to see you, too." The voice was only a hoarse whisper as he nodded at the chair beside his bed. "Sit down. You must be tired after your long trip."

Reno sat down and held his hat, turning it nervously in his hands. He was not good with sick people, and he never knew how to conceal his uneasiness.

Martin Reynolds said, "I'm sorry to have to call on you, but I have no one else."

Reno said quickly, "That's all right, Major. I'll be glad to do what I can." All the time he was wondering what he could do. Reynolds was obviously a wealthy man, and from the looks of the house, he was doing even better in Chicago than he had done in the South before the war. He said carefully, "I'm sorry to find you in such poor shape."

Reynolds waved his bony hand and shook his head. "It comes to all of us, I suppose, but it caught me off guard. I thought I had a few years left but—well, this thing is fast working." He stopped and looked at Reno. "I think it would have been better to catch a minié ball than to go through this, Jim."

"I'm sorry, sir."

"Well, well, never mind about me. Tell me what you've been doing."

Reno began giving a quick sketch of his life since he'd gotten out of the army, and finally he said, "And we hit it lucky in Alder Gulch. My two partners and I are making a pretty good thing out of it."

He saw as he talked that Reynolds was suffering intensely, although he said nothing. There was a light of pain in his eyes and his lips tightened, and once again Jim felt totally helpless.

"Jim," Reynolds said, "I don't know how much time I've got, so I'm not wasting any. Let me tell you why I've sent for you. But before I do, I want you to know that I've got no claim on you. I'm no longer your commanding officer. You've got a life to live, and if you can't do what I ask, then I'll think no less of you." He paused as Reno just sat waiting. Finally he continued, "This is a rich man's house, but I'm not a rich man. I used to be, but things have changed." He hesitated, then went on, "After the war I hit it big in investments, but I found out that in the stock market you can come down just as fast as you can go up." He went on talking about how he had gotten involved in the market and then how he made some bad investments. Reynolds then took a deep breath and said, "But it's all over now, Jim."

Reno looked around the room, at the heavy, expensive furniture and the ornate chandelier and asked quietly, "It's all gone, Major?"

"All gone. Everything I had before the war, everything after—even this house. There's a mortgage on it for more than it's worth."

"I've got some money, Major," Reno said at once. "I don't know how much it would cost to get you out—"

"More than you've got, Jim, and I wouldn't take it anyway. I got myself into this, and I'm not dragging anybody else down."

"I don't look at it that way, sir."

Once again a fire glowed in Reynolds' dull eyes, and he smiled. "I knew you'd say that, Jim. It's like you—but it won't do. There's one thing you can do, if you will. At least, I think you could." Doubt came over his face then, and his hands trembled. He had been a man of such power and such authority that it was hard for Jim to watch him as he wavered.

"What is it, Major?" he asked quickly. "I'll do it if a man can do it at all."

"All right, I'll tell you," Reynolds said. Then his voice picked up a little. "I'm going to lose this house, and there's no money left. My family will be out on the street, although they don't know that yet. But there's one thing I've got that I never put any paper on, that I never mortgaged. It's a piece of land out in Wyoming, a place called the Sun Ranch. I bought it quite a while ago and had it stocked. Always had the idea of going out there, getting away from the city, but my wife and family never liked the idea. They wouldn't go. I had to go by myself a few times, but it's been a few years."

A sudden spasm of pain gripped him. He clenched his teeth together, and Jim saw his hands tighten on the bedsheet. He watched helplessly until the spasm was gone and Reynolds took a deep breath. "That's all I've got, Jim, and I'm not even sure I've got that. A lot of it's on free grass, except for the home ranch itself. My foreman tells me that the neighboring ranches out there run over my range, and there's nothing much he can do about it. There's an awful bunch of pirates out there—land grabbers."

Reno nodded. "Yes, sir. I've seen it happen." His mind worked quickly and he said, "You want me to look into it for you?"

"I want you to do more than that, Jim. I want you to take my family out there, take care of them, and do whatever has to be done to put the ranch in good shape." He smiled grimly at Reno. "Not asking much, is it? For you to give up your life and take up my responsibilities?" Reynolds seemed to be in thought for a moment and then added, somewhat embarrassed, "And I was too proud to accept your money!"

Reno said with no hesitation, "I'll do it, Major. I'll do the best I can. I don't know the whole situation, but it could be pretty tough."

His ready agreement affected Reynolds deeply. He looked out the window, and his lips were trembling, Jim saw. Finally he cleared his throat and said hoarsely, "It's a thing I saw in you when you were just a boy, as wild a boy as I ever saw. Ready to win the whole war. I watched you all through that war, and there never was a better soldier or a better sergeant. And I saw another thing—you never let your friends down." He looked down at his thin frame lying under the sheet and said, "I never thought I'd come to this, and I hate to ask you, Jim, but you're my last hope."

Jim Reno was moved. He was not a man subject to much emotion, at least outwardly. But suddenly a love for his old friend and commander came to him. He reached over and put his hand on one of Major Reynolds', and the old man held on tightly. Reno's throat was tight, and he had to blink as his eyes grew misty. "I don't know what I can do, Martin," calling him for the first time ever by his first name. "But I'll do everything I can. And with God's help, I'll take care of your family."

Major Martin Reynolds held on to Jim's strong, tanned hand, looking down. Finally he raised his head, looked into Jim's eyes, and whispered, "Thank God you've come. You were my only hope, and the only hope for my family. I know God brought you here, Jim."

# THREE

*An Evening in Chicago*

Lillian Reynolds waited until just before dinner to tell the children that they would have company. "A friend of your father's is having dinner with us tonight," she said.

Chris Reynolds groaned. "Oh, no! Not another one of his old army cronies, I hope." Chris was seventeen and had draped his lean six-foot frame over a chair in the library. He had brown hair, brown eyes, and was a handsome young man by any standards. He was also, as his father was very much aware, spoiled and rebellious. "The last one he had that came by here bored me to death with all his old stories about how he almost won the war."

"I'm afraid he is an acquaintance of your father's from the war," Lillian said. "I hope you'll be nice to him." She hesitated, then said, "Your father was very glad to see him. I haven't seen him so lively in weeks."

Ramona Reynolds was sitting in an overstuffed horsehide chair, running her fingers through her hair. She was three years older than Chris and had the same good looks. Her hair was auburn with glints of red in it, and she had large brown eyes set off in her oval face. "I hope you don't expect us to sit around and entertain him, Mother," she said languidly. "We're going out tonight with Leon."

"No, I wouldn't ask you to do that, but you need to go see your father before you leave." Lillian smiled at them fondly.

She was a pretty woman and well accustomed to the better things of life. Her husband's illness had put a stop to many of her social activities, and there was a dissatisfied look in her expression. She had been born into a wealthy family, her father being an investor in the railroads, and had been highly sought after by many young men. But it was Martin Reynolds, a young up-and-coming Southerner in Chicago on business, who stole her heart. They married and moved to Richmond, where they intended to raise a family. When the war broke out, Martin joined the Confederate army, serving in his home state's Third Arkansas division. Lillian and the children moved back to Chicago to live with her parents, thus keeping them safe until after the war. After Appomattox Martin returned to Chicago and stayed, rather than submitting his family to the devastation that was the South, something his wife would not have been able to cope with. Shortly after the war, Lillian had risen rapidly to become one of the leaders of the Chicago social world. But now she bore the marks of a woman who had time on her hands.

"All right, Mother," Ramona said. "C'mon, Chris, we'd better go do that now. We'll want to make our escape as soon as possible after supper." She led the way, and the two of them went upstairs to see their father. Ramona sat on his bedside and teased him, trying to cheer him up. She was aware that he was very ill, but never referred to his illness. She chose to try to make him laugh and usually was successful. Tonight, however, he was depressed, and they left the room after fifteen minutes, promising to come back the next day. As soon as they were out of earshot, she shook her head. "He's not feeling at all well tonight, Chris. I think that doctor had better come up with some new kind of medicine."

They walked back down the hall and were met by their mother, who said, "Come along, it's time for dinner. Our guest is here." Turning, she walked before them, entered the smaller of the two dining rooms of the old mansion, and nodded to the man who rose to his feet as they came into the room. "These are my children, Mr. Reno. This is Ramona, and this is Chris. Children, this is Mr. James Reno."

Ramona was somewhat startled by the appearance of the man. She had expected someone her father's age, and she took in the youthful face of their guest with guarded surprise. *Why, he's not at all bad looking,* she thought. *I didn't know Father knew any young soldiers.* She said, "I'm glad to know you, Mr. Reno. Your visit has been good for Father, Mother tells me."

Reno nodded at the girl and shook the hand of the young man, then said quietly, "I'm sorry to see him in such poor shape."

"Well, let's sit down and eat," Lillian said smoothly. She motioned them to the table. "You can sit here, Mr. Reno." As they sat down she said, "I'm sorry, but the children have an engagement after dinner."

"I don't want to be a bother," Reno said. He was aware that the two younger members of the Reynolds family were examining him carefully. The thought came to him: *They were expecting something different, I guess.*

He said very little as the meal went on, although Chris

and Ramona tried to draw him out. Chris, especially, was interested in him, having read a great deal about the West. "So you're from the Wild, Wild West," he said jovially as he ate the steak that was placed in front of him by the maid. "How come you're not wearing two guns and a big tall hat? And woolly chaps? I thought all cowboys came rigged like that."

"Too much gear to bring to the big city," Reno said, smiling. "I'll put 'em on as soon as I get back to Montana."

"Do you really carry a gun?" Chris asked curiously.

Reno was uncomfortable with the boy's question. "Sometimes," he said as he shrugged. "Most of the time a gun just gets in your way. I wouldn't believe everything you read in those books. Most of them have been written by people who've never been west of the Mississippi."

Lillian felt that Chris was a little too forward and determined to move the conversation to more acceptable subjects. "Mr. Reno is in the gold mining business," she said. Then she turned to look at their guest, saying, "I'm sure that must be fascinating—and very profitable, too, I hope."

Reno smiled at her. "Well, fascinating, maybe, but mostly it's a lot of hard work for just a little money, unless you strike it big." At her urging he began to tell them about the mining camp at Alder Gulch.

While he talked, Ramona listened carefully. She took in the clean-cut features, the steady black eyes set in the wedge-shaped face, and was favorably impressed. His hands, she saw, were very brown and square, and looked tremendously strong. He was not a large man, not as tall as Chris, but he had a strong-looking upper body and seemed more graceful than she expected a cowboy to be.

After dinner, when they rose from the meal, an impulse

took her. "Why don't you come out with us, Mr. Reno? See a little bit of Chicago while you're here. We're going to a rather interesting place." A smile turned the corners of her mouth upward, and humor was in her dark eyes. "We're going to a place that might make you feel more at home—one of the rougher sides of Chicago."

"Yes," Chris joined in with a grin, "kind of like your Wild West, I guess. Go strap on your gun and come along with us."

"Guess I'll just stay and talk to your father." Reno had risen to his feet. Smiling at Lillian Reynolds, he said, "That was a fine meal, Mrs. Reynolds. I appreciate it." He nodded at Chris and Ramona, saying, "Have a good time," and turned and left, heading for Martin Reynolds' room.

When he got there, he found Martin very tired and sleepy. "That medicine Lillian gave me has just about worn me out," he said groggily. "It's good for the pain, but it just puts me out of it."

Reno sat down in the chair by his bed and said, "I just met your son and daughter, Martin. They're fine-looking young people."

A look of dissatisfaction came into Martin Reynolds' hooded eyes as he answered. "They look all right, but I've done a poor job of raising them, Jim. A poor show."

"Why, they seem fine to me. What's wrong with them?"

"Spoiled rotten, that's what's wrong with them," Martin growled. "I've given them everything they wanted—which was a mistake. It's the hard things that make a man and a woman what they ought to be, not the easy things. If I had it to do over again—" Suddenly he stopped and set his mouth in a tight line and grunted, "Always the sucker's cry: 'If only I'd done such and such.' I never thought I'd come to that, but I have." He lay there, his skeletal body still under the sheet, and the lines of pain that Reno had noticed earlier were even more pronounced. "Basically," he said, "they've got something good in them, both of them. But it'll never come out until they get tried."

Jim listened quietly as Martin spoke of his son and daughter, and he identified the hopeless longing in the sick man's voice. *He wants to do something to help his family,* he thought, *but it's too late now. And I don't know if I can help him with this.*

Then Reno said, "Well, I guess a man wants the best for his children. And if they've got something in them, it'll come out." He hesitated, then said again, "I'll do the best I can for them, Martin."

A warm light kindled in the sick man's sunken eyes, and he nodded, saying, "That's the most any man could do. I trust you more than I trust any other man, Jim." He was growing sleepier; his eyelids were drooping. "Guess I'm dropping off," he said. "You go ahead and get out of here now. I'll see you tomorrow."

"Good night, Martin." Reno got up and left the room, closing the door softly. When he got to the foyer he found that Ramona Reynolds was waiting for him. She was very attractive in her gray silk dress. Her hair was piled high on top of her head in current fashion, and she was smiling for him. "We're not going to let you go," she insisted with a smile. "You don't know anyone else in town, do you? No, I thought not. So you're coming with us, then, and we'll show you a little bit of Chicago's night life."

At that moment the brass knocker sounded, and she said, "That must be Leon now." She turned and went to the door, and as she left Chris came to stand beside Reno.

"That's Sis's best beau," he stated. "Leon Statler. He's done everything but haul Mona off to the altar, and I guess he'll get her sooner or later."

The man that came in the door was very large, six feet, two inches at least, with a heavy, muscular frame. He had blonde hair and pale blue eyes. Ramona brought him forward, saying, "Leon, this is Father's friend Jim Reno. Mr. Reno, this is Leon Statler."

A speculative light leaped into Statler's eyes, and he put forth a meaty hand. "Glad to meet you, Reno," he said pleasantly.

Reno took his hand and nodded, saying, "Yes, I'm glad to meet you too, Mr. Statler." At that moment he felt the powerful hand of the other man close in on his and was aware that the big man was putting all of his force into the handshake. Statler liked to prove his strength by crushing the hands of other men. Reno instantly tightened his own hand and the two men stood motionless.

Chris shifted his eyes to his sister and caught her glance, for they had seen Statler do this before. It was a trait that Mona did not like in Statler, and she had brought him to task before for bullying others with lesser strength. Now she felt sorry as she watched the two men, Reno looking almost diminutive beside the bulk of Statler.

Statler had a slight grin on his face and, being accustomed to easy victories, had no thought but that he would bring Reno into submission. But somehow it wasn't working. The hand of the smaller man did not give way as he expected. Instead, Reno's fingers were closing around his with a steely strength that seemed to bite into his flesh. The smile disappeared from Statler's face, and his lips grew tight. He threw all of his strength into his grip, but the bands that Reno seemed to have thrown around his hand grew tighter. He felt his hand giving way and gasped slightly. He had never met a man who could best him at this, and he could not believe what was happening.

Both Chris and Ramona were aware of the game that was going on and had expected to see Reno cringe and cry out as other men had. Instead, Mona saw, the face of Jim Reno was without strain. He was even smiling slightly, and his eyes were almost sparkling as he studied the face of the larger man. The silence went on, broken only by the labored breathing of Statler. Suddenly he wrenched his hand back and flexed the fingers, and stood there staring at Reno.

Chris laughed boisterously. "Well, Leon, I guess you won't try that trick anymore! Not with Reno, anyway."

Statler flexed his fingers again, looking at his hand as if it had betrayed him. Then he took a deep breath, and a smile came to his lips, though it did not reach his eyes. "I never met a man with a grip as good as yours, Reno," he said carefully. "I'll have to be careful picking my victims in the future. How'd you get a grip like that?"

"Hard work, I guess. Poking cows and digging in the ground with a pick. That gives a man a pretty good grip," Reno said casually.

He was uncomfortable with the three staring at him so intently, and he was glad when Ramona said, "Well, let's go. We're going to be late." She smiled warmly at Reno. "Maybe it's a good thing we've got you along, Jim, in case some thugs jump us."

★ ★ ★

The hour was late as the four exited from a saloon on the west side of Chicago. It had been a long evening, and they had visited several of the dives in that section of town. Leon Statler had been the guide and had taken them to two or three places that Jim felt no woman of character should enter, but he had said nothing. Statler and Chris Reynolds had imbibed rather freely of the liquor that flowed in all of these places. Jim himself had drunk only a few beers to be social and found it interesting that Ramona had barely touched the one drink that Statler had forced on her.

As they left the saloon, Reno looked up and saw that the skies were velvety black, and only one star gleamed faintly in all that expanse of ebony. As they walked along the street, their steps echoed hollowly on the cobblestones. Statler was talking about a prize fight he had seen in New York recently, and the others listened. They had reached an alley that intersected the street when a voice suddenly said, "Hold it right there!"

At once Reno turned, narrowed his eyes, and saw four men file out of the alley, all roughly dressed. Forming a semicircle in front of them, the leader—a man at least as tall and bulky as Statler himself—said, "Well, ain't this nice. We got us a party! Ain't we, guys?"

Another member of the band, a small man with a cap pulled low over his face, the lower part of which was covered by a full beard, said, "Yeah, Mack! And ain't it nice of them to ask us to join in with them?"

Statler looked at the thugs and said, "You fellows better move along before I call the police."

A laugh went up from all four of the men, and the one called Mack said, "Police? You're not uptown now, buddy!" He took a step closer and said in a threatening voice, "Now, about this party we're gonna have. We may need a little extra cash to finance it."

The threat in his rough voice was obvious, and Ramona stepped closer to Statler and took his arm. She had never been in a situation like this, and fear was a thread that ran along her nerves. She sensed also that Chris was sobered up by the situation, for he stood there without saying a word.

Statler, however, was not intimidated. He took one step forward and said, "Look, we don't want any trouble, but I can give you some if you want it." He doubled up one big fist and held it up, saying, "I'll take you one at a time."

Mack's big face was outlined by the yellow glare of the street lamps that flickered down the way. He had a bruiser's face, his features dulled by many blows and scarred with the marks of an ex-pug. "Ain't that nice," he said sarcastically. "Bully boy here's gonna give me a chance to fight all fair and square! That's the way they do it uptown, Sully. Watch the gentleman carefully—he's come to educate us heatherns."

The smaller man named Sully laughed shrilly. "Ain't that a sight!" He looked around at the other two and said, "Whaddya think, fellas? Want to fight him fair and square?"

One of the other men put a hand beneath his coat and came out with a knife that flickered coldly as it caught the glare of the lanterns. "This is the way I fight," he snickered. "What about the rest of you?"

All three of the others reached into their pockets and pulled knives out. "That's what they call us—the Night Blades," Mack, the leader, said, laughing quietly. "I used to do a little fighting in the ring, but I've given all that up." He waved the knife in a short half-circle and his voice lost the mocking tone. "All right, I've had enough fun with you. Let's have it."

Statler stood, eyes wide. He was not afraid of any man's fist, but the sight of those four knives was enough to stop him dead in his tracks. He said weakly, "Wait . . . now wait just a minute."

"Wait nothing!" Sully snarled. "Give us the coin, and maybe we'll let you go without carving our initials in you." Then his eyes went to Ramona, and he took a step toward her. "Maybe if I decorated Missy's face here a little bit, you swells would be a little quicker with the cash." He held his knife up and was about to advance, saying, "C'm'ere, missy, I've got a—"

"You fellas better scratch for it."

Mack blinked. Reno had suddenly stepped forward and was standing in front of his three companions. Mack glanced at the low-crowned, broad-brimmed black hat, the string tie, and the boots. "Well, cowboy, what brings you to Chicago?"

Reno said quietly, "Move along, and take the rest of the buzzards with you. I wouldn't want any of you to get hurt."

A laugh ran around the group, and Mack played to his audience. "You fellas watch this. I want to show you how to handle a Wild West cowboy." He held the knife up and said, "You got anything like this in your hip pocket, cowboy?"

Reno pushed his hat back with his right forefinger and then suddenly, as he reached down, a gun appeared in his hand. "No," he said pleasantly, "I don't have a knife."

A silence fell over the four, and then Sully said, "Wait, now—"

"No waiting, fellas," Reno said, and his voice had a hard edge to it. "Get along with you, now, and there won't be any trouble."

Mack's face grew ugly, and he snarled, "He won't use that gun. He can't get us all." He held the knife up and said, "I'm gonna cut your ears off. You won't use that—"

Suddenly an explosion pierced the night. Mack let out a small cry and dropped the knife, which clattered on the street. He reached up to grab his head, and even in the semidarkness, Mona could see that his ear had been struck by Reno's bullet.

Reno waved the gun and said, "Drop those knives, boys, and get on your way." Sully at once threw his knife down and the others followed suit. The suddenness of the shot and the deadliness in Reno's dark face convinced them.

Mack stared, brought his hand in front of his face, looked at the blood that stained it, and opened his mouth. But at that moment Reno turned his body slightly, extending his right arm, leaving Mack to stare straight into the barrel of a .44. Mack turned without a word, and the four of them disappeared, scrambling down the dark alley.

Reno slipped the gun back into his trouser band, pulled his coat back around him, and turned to study the other three. "Well, it's getting late. Don't you reckon we better get home?" He saw the shock written on the faces of all three and shrugged. "Yeah, I've seen the big city. It's pretty wild all right. But I guess I've seen enough excitement for one night. Shall we go, Miss Reynolds?"

Mona felt his hand take her arm. Her knees were weak, and she didn't know if her voice would work. She swallowed hard and whispered, "Yes, I—I think we'd better go." As they moved down the street she tried to understand her father's mysterious and unusual friend.

# FOUR
## "He's All You Have to Lean On"

"I've got to tell them, Jim," Martin Reynolds whispered. He was lying back on his pillow, and Reno sat beside him, leaning forward to catch the faint whisper of the dying man's voice. He'd been around death enough to know when it was near, and he had seen his friend go downhill more and more every day for the past two weeks. There was nothing he could do, of course, and he had learned that the family had resented Martin's clinging more and more to Reno as the end drew near.

"I guess you better make it clear, Major," Reno said quietly. "It's going to be a rough time for them, and they need to know what's happening."

"Go get them," Martin said, his voice growing stronger. "I should have told them all before this. I've tried to hint around about it, but I haven't had the nerve to tell them how bad things are. But it's time. Go now, Jim."

Reno left the room and found Lillian Reynolds in the library, writing at a desk. "Mrs. Reynolds," he said, "would you please come to your husband's room? He has something to tell you." He hesitated, then said, "He wants the children, too. Are they here?"

Lillian looked up, a startled look in her eyes. "Why, yes," she said. "They're in the parlor. I'll get them."

Reno went back to Martin's room and entered, saying, "They'll be right here, Martin."

The old man did not answer but tried to pull himself up in the bed. "Help me up, will you, Jim? Can't stand, but at least I want to sit up while I'm giving them this grief."

Reno walked over and carefully lifted the thin, emaciated body into a sitting position, propped him up with pillows, then moved back to take his stand against one of the walls.

A few minutes later Lillian Reynolds entered, followed closely by Chris and Ramona. "What is it, dear?" she asked with concern. "Are you bad? Do you want some more medicine?"

Martin Reynolds opened his eyes fully and said, "Medicine's no good now. I want to talk to you three—and it's not going to be pleasant."

Lillian glanced at Chris and Mona, and the three began to be alarmed. "What is it, Dad?" Mona asked, coming to stand beside him. "Is something wrong?"

Martin looked up into her face, and then as Chris and Lillian came to the other side of the bed he nodded. "Yes, something's wrong. Been wrong for a long time, and I just haven't been man enough to tell you about it."

Mona reached out, took his hand, and held it. She was shocked at the fragility of it. She could see that life was running low in her father. It had taken her a long time to accept this, but she had known now for days that he was dying and that nothing could stop it. She loved her father, and even as she held his wizened hand, she knew a thread of fear as she thought of a future without him. He'd always been there to help, and she knew well that she had not been a good daughter to him. But it was too late for that now. She merely said, "Go ahead, Dad, we're listening."

Reno lounged against the wall, his arms crossed and his head bent, looking at the floor. The thready voice of Major Martin Reynolds droned on for a long time, and Reno was aware that he was at last laying all of his troubles before his family. He told them how he had made bad investments, that he had had bad advice, and that, in an attempt to regain his fortune, he had borrowed against all they had, hoping to recoup. Then he said finally, "But it's all gone. Not only is the money gone, everything is gone. I mortgaged everything we have, hoping to make enough to take care of you."

Reno looked up and saw the pain etched in Reynolds' face and would have given anything to have given some consolation to the dying man.

"But—but surely not *everything!*" Lillian gasped. "You can't mean it's *all* gone, Martin!"

"Yes. That's exactly what I mean, Lillian," Martin said bitterly. "And here I am, dying, and not able to do a thing about it."

Chris began to ask specific questions about funds and about businesses that he was aware his father had been investing in. But Martin shook his head. "No, no, Chris, it's all gone, don't you understand? The creditors will come on you like wolves on helpless sheep. My lawyer has held them off as long as possible. You'll be left with the clothes you stand in, and that's all!"

Lillian Reynolds began to cry. This, Reno saw, hurt Martin tremendously. "I'm sorry, Lillian," he whispered. "It's all my fault. I'm a failure."

It was Mona who kissed the hand she held and said, "Don't you worry, Dad. We'll make out. We're strong, and we'll do fine." Her voice was not steady, and Reno, as well as the others, heard the uncertainty, fear, and doubt that ran through it. There was a smile fixed on her face, but it was not firm at all.

Her words, however, brought a little hope to Martin Reynolds, and he summoned a smile and patted her hand. "I'm glad you said that, daughter, real glad. Because now that I've given you the bad news, I've got one bit of good news to give you. Reno, come over here." Reno reluctantly left the wall and came to stand at the foot of the bed. He did not look at the others but kept his eyes on Martin's wan, pallid face. "You've been wondering why I've been sticking so close to Jim, and now I'm going to tell you. He's all you have to lean on, Lillian. And you too, Chris and Mona."

Reno flushed as the three turned to look at him with various forms of astonishment. An astonishment, he noticed, not unmixed with resentment.

Martin saw it too, and his voice grew stronger. "Don't look at him like that. He's here because I asked him to come. He's the only hope I've got for doing anything for you." A light came into his eyes that reminded Reno of the days when they had been in battle together, when the spirit of Martin Reynolds had kept the whole company going. There was life still in the man, and he mustered it all up as he said, "I didn't tell the complete truth a minute ago. There is one thing left."

"What's that, Father?" Chris asked at once, his eyes alert.

"A few years ago I bought a ranch out in Wyoming. I've tried to talk to you about it, but none of you were really interested. I've hung on to it all these years and tried to keep it going, and it's still there."

"There's no mortgage on it, Dad?" Mona asked quickly.

"Not a penny—it's all free and clear!"

"Why, it'll be all right then!" Mona spoke with relief. "We can sell the ranch and surely buy a little house or something here in Chicago." She patted her father's hand and said, "I'm glad you didn't mortgage it, Dad."

"Wait a minute," Martin said quickly. "It's not that simple. Let me try to explain it to you." He went on to outline the problem: "Except for the house and a small bit of land, the rest of it's free range. I intended to buy more some day, but never got to."

"But it's worth something, isn't it?" Lillian asked fearfully. The idea of a moneyless future seemed to have paralyzed her. She had never known anything like this, and she held on to Chris tightly.

"That's what you've got to understand," Martin said gently. "That ranch has been held together by a foreman, and the ranchers around it are the worst bunch of pirates you ever saw. They've taken a lot of it already, the graze I used to have, and now they're just waiting to take the rest."

"But the law can do something—"

"No, the law won't do anything. It's not Chicago, Lillian," Martin answered firmly. Then he looked up again and nodded at Jim. "Jim Reno is the only hope we've got, any of us. It'll take a man strong enough to go in and stand against everything they'll throw at him, and Jim has agreed to do it. I hated to ask—you know how I hate to ask for favors—but I had to."

The three stared again at Reno, and already he could see in their eyes that they didn't like putting their well being and their fate in the hands of a stranger. He said nothing, but kept his eyes fixed on Martin.

The crisis had pulled what little strength Martin Reynolds had down to a low ebb. His eyes began to flutter. "I wish I could do more," he said, "but I can't." He looked up at Chris and Mona and said wistfully, "I wish I'd taught you to stand on your own. But it's not too late. The West can do that for you. Stick with Jim—stick with him—"

Lillian saw he was falling asleep and quickly moved around and arranged the pillows, laying his head down on one of them. Then she turned and said to her children, "Your father doesn't have the strength to say any more. We'd better let him rest."

The four of them left the room, and as soon as they were outside Jim said evenly, "I know this is hard for you. But I just want you to know that I love and respect Martin Reynolds more than any other man. And I'm here to do whatever I can for him, and for you."

"Thank you," Lillian said weakly. Here was someone she could lean on; there was no one else in sight. "I don't know what to do, I don't know how we can live, I—I just don't know—"

"Don't worry, Mom," Chris said, coming to stand beside her. "We'll make it, won't we, Sis?"

Mona said, "Yes, of course, Mother. We'll be all right." Then she looked at Reno, and he saw the pride in her eyes. It was obvious that she hated to lean on anyone, and her voice was even as she said, "I'm sorry that we have to call on you for help. We've never had to do it before."

Reno studied the girl with care, noting her proud look and straight carriage. Then he said, "We all come to that sooner or later, asking for help." Then he nodded slightly. "And none of us ever learns to like it."

★ ★ ★

The funeral was simple, and a larger crowd than Reno had expected was there. He stayed in the background, watching as the family came, dressed in black. He followed them out to the cemetery and was glad that it was a bright day, the first day of May. Funerals on cloudy, stormy days had always seemed to him the worst thing in the world. He had been in the room when Martin Reynolds had died, and one of the last things the dying man had said was, "Jim, you've made this so much easier for me. I know I can trust you."

The words of the dying man were something Reno treasured, for he had wanted the respect of his old commander, and yet at the same time they were a heavy weight upon him. He knew the cattle country and knew what lay ahead for the Reynolds family if they tried to reclaim Sun Ranch. It would be a battle, and it would take everything he had to pull them through. But he said nothing of this to the family.

Two days after the funeral he accompanied the family to the office of the lawyer, a tall man named Henry Jones. Jones put them at their ease and then proceeded to go through the legal terminology that lawyers seemed to feel necessary. His face was somber as he read. When he was through he looked at the family with a hint of regret, placed the paper he was reading on his desk, and covered it with his hand. He hesitated and looked carefully at the family. "I'm sorry to have to give you this news. But I suppose Mr. Reynolds went over all of it with you."

Mona spoke up. "What it means is that there's nothing left. Is that right, Mr. Jones?"

Jones bit his lip and nodded. "Yes, that's what it means, I'm afraid, Miss Reynolds. I wish I could do something, but it's out of my hands."

"What about the furniture? The carriages? Are they gone too?" Lillian asked tremulously.

"I'm afraid so. Your husband had many debts, and I regret to say that most of your possessions will have to be sold to pay them off. Anything left over, of course, would belong to you and your family." Jones again hesitated, then clasped his fist and struck the paper on the desk. "Blast it, I wish I could do something, and I hate to put this on you. But I have to tell you that you'll have to think about moving pretty soon. The truth is, I've put off the creditors just about as long as I can. Foreclosure on your property can't be avoided any longer. You have a week at the most."

The news seemed to hit the Reynoldses hard. They were homeless, and they had never faced anything like this before. There was a weakness in them that they tried to cover, and Mona managed to say, "Well, we're leaving for Wyoming anyway, for the property there."

Jones seemed relieved and said quickly, "I'm glad you decided to go. It's probably for the best, and I wish you well." He looked at Reno and continued, "I had several talks with Martin before he died about you, Mr. Reno. He put a lot of confidence in you. So if I can be of any help—"

"Thank you," Reno said, knowing well that the lawyer could be of no help in what lay ahead of them. "I'll let you know if there's anything."

They left the lawyer's office and went back to the house. Lillian said as they entered, "Jim, we'd better talk."

"All right, Mrs. Reynolds." He followed her along with the children to the parlor.

Lillian sat down and looked at him. Her mouth was tight, and she was very pale. "There's no sense putting this off," she said. "When can we leave?"

Reno blinked. He was surprised at the determination the woman was showing. He had not expected it from her. "Why," he said carefully, "that'll be up to you. But I don't see any need to hang around here."

"Very well then. We'll arrange for Mr. Jones to sell our personal possessions and settle the debts. Will you arrange for the transportation, Jim?"

"Why, Mother," Mona said in surprise, "we can't be ready that quickly!"

"Why not?" Lillian demanded. Now that she had taken the plunge, she was anxious to get it done. "We can only take what we can carry in our suitcases—and that's about all we have anyway," she added. "Mr. Jones can wire us the profits from the sales—if there are any."

Chris wasn't happy about it. "Why don't you and Mona stay here, Mother? I'll go with Jim, and we'll get things ready. We'll get you a room or something."

"That might be best, Mrs. Reynolds," Reno put in. "It's going to be pretty rough where we're going, and we don't know what we'll run into. Why don't Chris and I—"

"No," Lillian said firmly. "We're all going together. It's what Martin wanted, and it's all I see to do. We all go together." Then she said, "And you may as well call me Lillian. It looks like you're a member of the family now."

Mona glanced at Reno, who caught her eyes. There was a clash between them for one moment, and finally Mona said, "Certainly Mother and I are going." She spoke stiffly and could not bring herself to acknowledge her debt to Reno again.

Instead she said, "We'll get this ranch settled as quickly as possible, and then you won't have to bother with us anymore."

Reno knew it would not be like that, but this was no time to argue. He said, "I'll get the train tickets, and we'll leave the day after tomorrow."

A silence fell on the room, and all four of them knew that the future was highly uncertain. Reno at least had an idea of the perils to come, but the Reynoldses were entering a world that was as alien to them as the far side of the moon. It was Lillian who said, "Well, Jim, we're in your hands now." Then she smiled and put her hand on his shoulder. "And let me say I don't think Martin could have found a better man to entrust us to!"

# FIVE
## The Stage to Banning

The three-day train trip from Chicago had taken most of the starch out of the Reynolds family. As they dismounted from the old wood burner, Jim took the hand of Lillian Reynolds, whose face was lined with fatigue. It was, he knew, not an experience that was common to the woman, for she had been spoiled, used to the good things, accustomed to having things done for her. And Reno had done the best he could to accommodate her, but the train that chugged across the prairie was not designed for the comfort of anyone accustomed to life's finer things.

He turned and was about to hand Mona to the ground, but she gave him an even look, held to the handhold on the train, and stepped to the ground by herself. She was followed by Chris, who got out and arched his back, saying, "Man, am I glad to get off of this thing! I feel like I've eaten a ton of cinders since we left Chicago!"

Reno smiled briefly, saying, "I hope you feel that good after a couple days on the stage." He turned, swept his eyes across Cheyenne, then nodded. "That looks like the stage station over there," he said. "You ladies go on over. Chris and I will get the luggage."

As the women plodded across the baked ground to the single-story wooden framed building flanked by corrals on both sides, he led Chris to the baggage car. The door slammed open, and a short, chunky, red-faced brakeman scrambled inside, asking their names. He started heaving baggage out recklessly, Jim and Chris catching it as best they could. Then he leaped to the ground, slammed the door shut, and hurried back to the caboose without a word. The two men picked up as much of the baggage as they could and started across to the stage station. When they were halfway there, the train gave a shrill blast and was off, chugging and disturbing the silence of the prairie with its cries.

Lillian and Mona stood waiting for them, and as the men put the suitcases down, Lillian said petulantly, "I hope there's a place to eat here." Then she glanced around at the wooden buildings scattered aimlessly, as if thrown by a giant over the prairie, and shook her head. A line formed around her mouth, and her eyes were rebellious. "But I don't think I'd feel safe eating anything in this place."

Reno said, "We'll get something," then entered the stage office. It was a single room with a battered oak desk at one end, behind which sat a man with a full complement of salt-and-pepper whiskers and a set of mild blue eyes.

"Catching the stage?" he inquired easily.

"Yes, we'll need four places," Jim said, then lowered his voice. "And we've got enough baggage to fill two stages."

The ticket agent grinned at him and nodded. "Well, we'll do what we can. These stages will only hold so much. Where're you going?"

"Banning."

The agent scratched his stomach and nodded. "Stage'll be in about noon," he remarked casually, "if it ain't late—which it usually is. You can get something to eat over there." He gestured vaguely across the street and to his right.

"Thanks."

Reno walked outside and said, "Stage'll be here in a few hours. Let's get something to eat." He walked along with Lillian. Although it was only nine o'clock, the sun was already beating down, baking the parched earth even harder. "It'll be hot today," he said. "Those stages get pretty sticky."

They went into the two-story building and found the first floor divided by a hall. On one side was a saloon, on the other side was a restaurant, neither of them over twenty feet square. A heavyset woman of mixed Indian blood came up to ask, "Something to eat?" She took in Reno's nod and said, "We got steak and potatoes and pie."

Reno glanced quickly at Mona and a grin touched his lips, which she resented. "I guess we'll have steak, potatoes, and pie," he said to the woman. "And anything you've got wet to drink."

"Hmph! Some breakfast!" Mona whispered not too softly to her mother.

They went into the room, and as they waited on the meal Chris looked around with distaste. "Not much like Delmonico's, is it, Mother?" He was wearing a fawn-colored suit that was wrinkled, creased, and speckled with stains from three days' hard travel. "How long will this trip take, Jim?" he asked.

"Best part of a couple days," Reno said, adding, "far as I understand it." He leaned back in his chair and listened as

Chris talked idly, wondering what would be the result of submitting these three tender and uninitiated citizens to the roughness of western life. He had seen it fail before and was not at all sure anymore if Martin Reynolds had made the right decision. But he knew, of course, that there was nothing else to do, so he determined to make the best of it.

The meal came—four steaks, greasy and tough, potatoes, pie, and water. Jim was hungry and wolfed his down. Chris ate half of his, and the two women only picked at their meal. Reno said nothing, knowing that it would be useless.

After the meal they sat and drank coffee, which was black as night and strong as coffee could be. Reno drank his slowly as they whiled away the time until the stage came.

At eleven-thirty Jim said, "Come on. We might as well walk back over to the stage office. It'll be late, I guess, but we might as well be there as here." He paid the waitress, and the four walked across the blistering, cracked earth. Though the walk was not long, they were glad to step up onto the porch into the shade. Several battered chairs lined the porch, and the women sat down while Jim and Chris leaned against the wall.

A buggy was coming across the countryside. Jim had seen the dust rising as they left the restaurant. It drew nearer, and he saw that it contained two passengers, a woman and a man. As it stopped immediately in front of the station he heard the woman say, "Thank you. You don't need to wait." As she proceeded to get out of the wagon, Reno moved forward and offered her his hand. He took part of her weight as she swung lightly down, and then stepped back.

She was a dark woman in a dust-gray dress with a bodice that strained against her full figure. She wore a small hat with a half veil on a mass of glossy black hair dropping in a long fall around her head. Her face was small and exact with clear features. The strong light shining against her made her close her eyes for a moment. Then she opened them and motioned toward the wagon. "Will you help me with my bags, please?" she asked. She spoke quietly, but there was a certain hardness in her voice.

"Sure," Reno said. He picked up two bags and said, "I'll get your trunk if you would like to see about your ticket." The woman left, and Reno moved to get the small trunk, placing it on the porch.

A few moments later the woman came out, and Chris said, "Here, ma'am, have a seat."

"Thank you." She nodded courteously, taking Chris in with one easy, smooth glance. "I'll be sitting a long time today. I think I'll stand."

"I'm Chris Reynolds. This is my mother, and my sister, Ramona."

"I'm Belle Montez," the woman said. She looked at Reno inquiringly.

He took his hat off, saying, "I'm Jim Reno, Miss Montez." He hesitated, then said, "You headed north?"

"Yes."

The brevity of her reply caught at all of them, and Jim, accustomed to the ways of the West where people did not speak freely of themselves, asked her nothing more. He looked up and motioned toward a curl of dust on the horizon. "Stage is coming." They waited as the stage pulled in and slammed to a halt. A hostler came to change the team.

The driver, a tall, skinny man who seemed to be made of dark leather, said briefly, "Pullin' out soon as the horses are changed. Get your stuff loaded."

Reno and Chris quickly began to pile the luggage into the boot and had to put several bags on top. Reno lashed them down with some rawhide thongs provided by the driver, and, thirty minutes later, with a new team in place, they were ready to go.

Jim helped the three women in, then climbed in himself. There were two other passengers in the coach. One was a short, heavyset man who announced that his name was Carlton, obviously a salesman or drummer of some sort. The other was a big man in buckskins who said, "I'm Al Jensen." The four men were crowding each other, trying to make room, and Jensen said, "I'll ride shotgun. Tired of this blamed coach anyway." He crawled out and climbed up with the driver; the coach gave under his weight, then settled back.

The driver called out, "Hup, Babe! Hup, Samson!" and the coach swayed, surged forward, and in a cloud of dust left the stage station.

The heat was oppressive, and they had not been underway for more than twenty minutes when Ramona began to feel the fine dust that filtered into the coach onto her face, and sweat began to collect on her brow. Taking out a handkerchief, she dabbed at her face carefully and managed only to smear the dust. Glancing at her mother, she saw that she was just as bad off. She settled down with resignation, saying nothing. She had grown angry on the train ride at the inconvenience and discomfort, but this was much worse. For the next five hours without a break the coach rolled along, the sand falling in ropes off the turning back wheels, the pale sun overhead baking and cooking the passengers inside. There was no wind, and the discomfort became something close to actual pain, but Mona was determined not to complain.

Reno put his hat down over his face, leaned his head back, and went to sleep. He was accustomed to taking his sleep in short spans, whenever and wherever he could get it, and he subconsciously rolled his weight with the swaying of the coach. When he awoke he saw that the sun was going down. He removed his hat, wiped his forehead, and grinned at Chris. "This heat's pretty bad," he said, "but it'll get cooler in an hour or two."

"I hope so. I'm about melted down," Chris said wearily.

An hour later they pulled into a stage stop, and the driver called out, "Stopped for the night! Leave at dawn!" Jim opened the door and jumped down. When Lillian appeared, he realized that she was worn out.

"Sorry about this, Lillian," he said. "I know it's rough, but it'll be better when we get to town."

She smiled feebly at him but said nothing; she was too tired to speak. Ramona stepped to the door, and this time when he lifted his hand, she took it. Stepping to the ground, she swayed for a moment with weariness. Then, after regaining her senses, she took her mother's arm, and they entered the stage station. Belle Montez came out, holding lightly to Jim's hand, looking up at him. She was not a tall woman, but was well formed. She asked curiously, "They're not your family?"

"No. I'm going to help them get settled near Banning."

"Banning? Why, that's where I'm going," she said. "To a ranch just outside Banning."

Jim turned with her, saying, "We'll be neighbors, then. The Reynoldses have a ranch in the valley."

The information did not seem to please the woman; there was an air of regret about her somehow. He had not seen her smile, and he wondered what was troubling her. She was an attractive woman, and her manner told him that she had experience with men. She looked at him straightforwardly, almost in a bold fashion, and yet she was not exactly the hardened type that he had seen in other places, at other times. He didn't question her.

They stepped inside the station and found that the rooming situation was simple. "Got two rooms," the station man said. "One for men and one for women."

Lillian said, "Anything. I'm so tired!"

"Take the room on the left, back down that hall. Supper will be ready in about half an hour."

Lillian looked at the small, dark woman and said, "Miss Montez, I guess we'll have to share the same room."

"Yes, I guess we will," Belle Montez said, nodding. She turned and walked down the hall, the other ladies accompanying her.

Reno and Chris moved over to the table and sat down, Chris speaking about the miles that lay ahead. Thirty minutes later the innkeeper's wife began bringing food to the table. She moved down the hall and called out brusquely, "Supper's ready! Come and get it!"

It was a cheerless meal, poorly prepared. Jim, who sat next to Belle, said, "Not much of a place."

She turned her head, her black eyes fixed on him steadily, and answered, "No, but it's the only place."

Jim liked her attitude. She was not a woman given to complaining, he saw, and nodded. "That's a good way to look at it. We have to take things like that, don't we. No matter how bad they get, I guess it doesn't do much good to argue about it. Or complain."

His remark touched her for some reason, he noticed. She

sat very still, holding her fine hands together. She had long, tapering fingers, beautifully shaped, and there was a smoothness to her cheeks as she thought over what he had said. She again fixed her eyes directly on his, and he was aware that behind their quietness there was a knowledge that he had not yet plummeted. "Yes. There's no sense complaining," she said almost in a whisper. "We have to do what we can." Then she gave him a small smile.

Reno broke his own rule and made a personal inquiry. "You have relatives in Banning?" At once he saw that the question disturbed her and wished he had not asked it. He amended, "Ah, I'm getting to be an old woman. Go around nosing in everybody's business. Forget it, Miss Montez."

Belle shrugged a little. "I'm going there to marry a man," she said briefly. She said no more, but rose from the table and went down the hall to the bedroom, and Jim saw that he had blundered into a part of her life that she was not comfortable with.

*What'd I ask a fool question like that for,* he asked himself. *I'm old enough to know better than to nose into people's business.*

He rose from the table, stepped outside, and took a walk for the better part of an hour, looking up at the stars and wondering what lay ahead. Finally he came back and played cards with the stage driver and Chris until bedtime. Then he said to Chris, "We better sleep if we can. Tomorrow won't be any easier."

Everyone rose the next morning before dawn. They ate a quick breakfast thrown together by the station manager's wife and rolled out when the gray edges of light were beginning to appear in the east. None of the passengers had much to say, and the Reynoldses endured the dust and the heat and the discomfort as stolidly as possible for the first few hours.

Reno tried to ease them by saying, "We ought to be there by three."

"I don't think this trip will ever end!" Mona said sharply. The dirt, dust, and heat had worn her so that her lips made a pale line on her face. She had grown terser and more irritable until finally Chris, who had tried to stay as pleasant as possible, stopped speaking to her. Lillian Reynolds had been reduced to silence and seemed to be gritting her teeth just to stay upright in the coach. Belle Montez had borne the trip better than the other women, obviously having traveled in such a fashion before. As the stage rolled along that morning, Reno stole a glance at her as she looked out the window, admiring the smooth cheeks, long eyelashes, and tiny, well-shaped ears with jade earrings dangling from them.

Belle had exchanged few words during lunch at a stage stop where they received fresh horses, revealing nothing of herself and not seeming to crave company. As they were boarding the coach again, a tall man covered with dust approached. He looked them all over good, taking off his hat as his eyes met Belle's. "Well howdy," he said, a wolfish grin breaking across his grimy face.

He looked up at the stage driver, who was biting off a chew of tobacco, lounging in his seat. "Got room for another passenger, Ed?"

The stage driver gave him a sour glance and nodded briefly. "Throw your saddle up here, Box." The tall cowboy took the saddle he'd been carrying and tossed it easily to the top of the coach. He had sinewy shoulders, a strong neck, and was dressed as an ordinary range rider. The only careful thing about his dress was the cartridge belt and holster around his waist.

"Lost my horse way back," he said, then turned his gaze again on Belle. He had a bold aspect to his face—a hawk nose and a pair of determined brown eyes. "Don't reckon we've met," he said. "My name's Lester Box." He waited, and when Belle did no more than nod, he moved closer, saying, "We don't get many of your kind around here, missy. You goin' in to Banning?"

Belle had sized him up at once and turned away to get in the stagecoach. Chris stood watching and stepped forward to help her. But the tall rider stepped forward suddenly, pushed him back, and took Belle by the arm. A shadow crossed his sharp face, and he demanded, "What's the matter? Ain't I good enough for you?"

Chris's face had flushed red, and he stepped forward and put his hand on Box's shoulder. He started to say something, but before he could speak, the tall cowpuncher had wheeled and struck him a blow in the chest that drove him backwards, a chilling blow that took his breath.

"Keep your hands off me, dude," Box said. He waited for one moment to make sure that Chris would make no other move, then turned to Belle, saying, "Now. Lemme help you up, little lady."

Belle drew back as the man put his hand out and snapped, "I don't need your help." She turned to climb into the stage, but Box's hand shot out and gripped her arm, pulling her back around.

"You're gonna like me after you get to know me better," he sneered. When she began to struggle, his teeth flashed white against his tan and he said, "I like 'em with a little life in 'em. What are you, some kind of Mexican senorita?"

At that moment a hand closed around his arm, and he

was pulled backwards so rapidly he lost his balance. At the same time he was given a shove and, trying to catch himself, he stepped on one of his spurs and fell sprawling to the ground. He stared up wildly at Jim Reno, who had supplied the momentum, and his face burned red. He scrambled to his feet and took one step toward Reno. He cursed and without warning threw a punch straight at Reno's face. When Reno moved his head to one side, Box fell forward; as he did so, he was struck a terrible blow in the midsection. The punch was short, but Reno had pivoted, throwing all of his weight into it. It doubled Box up, and he fell to the ground in a fetal position, gagging and gasping for breath.

Reno kept his eyes fixed on the man for a moment, then reached down, took the gun from his holster, and held it in one hand. He did not see the pale faces of the Reynolds women in the coach, nor did he see the admiration that came into the eyes of Belle Montez. He stood there waiting, and finally the man began to catch his breath. Reno reached down and hauled Box to his feet. When he was upright, he said, "You're not taking this stage. You'll have to take the next one."

He waited for Box to speak, and Box was very much aware of the gun in Reno's hand. "You can't leave me out here," he said finally. His eyes turned to slits. "No one's ever laid a hand on me! Whoever you are, I'll find you and kill you!"

"Your privilege to try. Now back off." Reno waved the gun at him, and as Box backed up, he helped Belle into the stagecoach. Chris scrambled in, then Reno stepped inside and shut the door. "I'll toss your gun out a hundred yards down the road," he said. The driver tossed Box's saddle to the ground as Reno said, "Let's go, driver."

The coach swayed as it began to move, and all the passengers had their eyes set on Reno. After a few moments he tossed the gun out unheedingly, then turned to face Belle. "I'm sorry you had to put up with that," he said.

"Thank you," she replied calmly. "He was . . . unpleasant." Then she added, "You'll have trouble with him. I know his kind—he won't rest until he tries to get his revenge."

Reno shrugged and then appeared to put the whole matter from his mind. But the others had been shocked by the sudden explosion that had come out of nowhere. Now as Mona watched Reno, who was staring out the window, she was thinking, *This is another kind of world we're in.* She glanced at her mother. *I wonder if she can stand it.* Then she thought quickly, *I wonder if any of us can.*

The stage rolled on, raising dust and throwing a high cloud into the sky. Finally, as the afternoon sun began to cast long shadows, they pulled into a small town, the stage creaking to a halt. "Everybody out!" the driver yelled. "Everybody out for Banning!"

# SIX
## A Man and a Woman

Dave Holly stepped off the porch of the Palace, Banning's only hotel, as the stagecoach rounded the corner. He angled across the street, moving slowly, his hazel eyes fixed on the swaying vehicle, his lips pulled tightly together. He was a man of average height, muscular, with heavy shoulders, and fair hair. Stepping up on the boardwalk, he moved until he was close enough to watch the passengers descend. He saw first a trim-looking man with a black hat and a light shirt, wearing a .44. This man reached back and handed down a woman who looked to be about fifty years of age, then a younger woman. Holly studied the younger woman carefully, then mentally passed over her. But when the third woman emerged, something different came into his face. He moved forward at once, removed his hat, and stood before her. "I'm Dave Holly," he said quietly. "You're Belle Montez, I take it."

Belle looked at him with composure, and he felt himself being analyzed by a quick mind. Her gaze disturbed him somehow, as did her appearance. He had not expected such an attractive woman, and to cover his confusion he put his hat on and took her arm, saying, "I'll take you into the hotel. I've got a room for you there."

Once inside the hotel, they went up the stairway that broke the middle of the hallway, coming to a room at the end of the second floor hallway. Pulling the key from his pocket, Holly opened the door and allowed Belle to enter. He said, "I'll give you time to freshen up, and I'll come back later."

"No," she said firmly, "it's all right. Come in." She moved across the room, taking in the furniture and the arrangements, and noted that he seemed very nervous as he came in. "Sit down," she said, gesturing to a chair.

"No," he said, and went to stand against a wall. The room seemed too small to him; her presence affected him strongly.

"I had you pictured in my mind," Belle said quietly, "and I'm not disappointed. It was thoughtful of you to meet me and to have the room ready."

"Well, it's awkward enough as it is," Holly said slowly. Then a slight smile touched his tough lips, and he shrugged his muscular shoulders. "I never thought I'd be doing a thing like this, finding a wife through the mails."

"How did you happen to write?" she asked.

Holly reached up, rubbed the scar on the right side of his chin thoughtfully, glanced at her, and said, "A friend of mine from Texas wrote. He told me about a girl that had gone there to marry a fellow who was gonna start a ranch, had saved up some money for it. He told me about how the fellow got killed before the girl got there, so she buried him. And you were the girl."

He watched carefully to see if his mention of this brought grief to her eyes, but she did not seem at all affected. "Was it pity that made you write?" she asked.

"No, no," he answered, "it wasn't that. My friend mentioned that you said a funny thing. He said that the country had cheated you, so you'd stay and take your pay for it somehow. Well," he cleared his throat and again looked nervous as he added, "I thought about that for a couple of months. Stuck in my mind what kind of girl you must be, so I wrote."

Belle said casually, "I wondered why you didn't come, instead of just writing."

Holly shrugged. "That wouldn't have done any good. Whatever it was you felt for the other fellow—well, I can't give you that. You buried something with him that no other man can get. But you said you'd stay in the country and lick it, and that stuck with me. So I wrote and offered you my prospects. A letter was best for that. I can write straighter than I can talk."

"Your letters were very straightforward. They said all the worst things first."

"I was only fair. There aren't many women here in the valley; it's a lonesome country. You'll never starve, and you'll never know harshness from me. But one thing I can't provide—and that's what the other man meant to you."

Belle was interested. She looked at him carefully but said nothing.

Then Holly continued, "I know my limits. I need a wife, and I can give you a place to live—a home. Maybe that'll be enough." He suddenly seemed embarrassed and showed it. He bit his lip, and his eyes roved nervously around the room. "Or maybe that won't be enough. This can be the turning point, Miss Montez. You've seen me, and it can end right here, if you wish."

Belle lifted her head, raising her chin high, as if she had heard a challenge. "People can't go back. They have to go on. I want something to show for my life." A thought came to her then, and she considered Holly, assessing him. "You're disappointed in me."

"Well, I expected less," Holly said awkwardly. "Somebody plain and practical, somebody used to not having a lot of money. I don't have much. The bargain," he added, "would be good for me, but bad for you."

Belle liked his straightforwardness and honesty, and she said, "I won't change my mind. I'm willing to marry you."

Her words caught Holly off guard. He had not expected such a quick answer, and it made him apprehensive. He didn't want her to see that he was uncertain, for he believed in keeping a bargain. Still, ever since she'd stepped off the stage and he'd seen her dark beauty and her worldly manner, he'd had his doubts. He said quickly, "I won't let you make up your mind right now. Stay in Banning for a week. You can put up here in the hotel. I'll see you every day, and by then you'll know for certain."

Belle knew what was in his mind. "I understand," she said quietly.

"I'll leave you to freshen up now. Suppose I come back about six. We'll have supper and can talk more."

"That will be fine, Mr. Holly. Or I guess we should call each other Dave and Belle now."

He nodded and tried to smile. "Yes, that would be better."

He turned and left the room without another word. Belle went to the window and watched as he left the hotel, angled down the street, and went into the Traildriver Saloon half a block away. She came back, sat slowly down in the chair, and bowed her head. Thoughts ran through her mind. *He sees what I've been. He knew at once, just by looking at me. Am I so trans-*

*parent? Will I ever find a man who won't look at me that way?*
Finally she rose, took off her hat, walked over to the wash-
stand, and began cleansing the trail dust from her face.

★ ★ ★

"How long will we have to stay here, Jim?" Lillian Reynolds
looked around the room, and Reno stopped as he was prepar-
ing to leave.

"Not more than a day," he answered. "We'll rent a rig in
the morning. I'm going down to the sheriff's office now to
make sure that the legal side of it's all taken care of. You can
have supper downstairs or in the restaurant down the street if I
don't get back in time. Or maybe you'd like to be alone."

"I'll go with you, Jim, if it's all right," Chris said eagerly.

"Sure." Reno nodded to the two women and left the hotel
room. Followed by Chris, he left the hotel and stopped someone to ask directions to the sheriff's office. It was a block and
a half away, and they discovered that the sheriff was out. "We'll
see him later. Might as well go back to the hotel and see if
your mother and sister want to go get something to eat."

They made their way back, and as they entered the hotel,
Reno noticed a group of men in the dining room to the right.
His eyes narrowed, and he moved over to the desk clerk and
asked, "Special kind of meeting going on in the dining room?"

The clerk, a thin middle-aged man with sandy hair,
glanced into the dining room and nodded. "Yes, that's some of
the ranchers. They're having some kind of a cattlemen's meeting, I think."

"Thanks." Reno turned and gave Chris a slight smile.
"Might as well introduce ourselves to the valley, Chris. But
somehow I don't think we're going to be very welcome."

Reno entered the dining room, followed closely by Chris, and at once was addressed by a huge man with a thatch of white hair. "You're in the wrong room. This is a private meeting," he said gruffly.

"Cattlemen's meeting?" Reno asked quietly.

"Yes. Move along," the big man said impatiently.

Reno glanced around the room, noting that these men were obviously owners, not just range riders. "I'm in the right place," he said.

"Representin' what outfit?" the big man demanded.

"Sun Ranch."

Reno's words broke on the quiet room and brought a wave of disturbance over it. It was obvious even to Chris that they were unwelcome. The big man said, "I'm Simon Meade. And you're still in the wrong room." He eyed Reno and Chris for a moment, then went on, "Pack Ganton represents Sun."

Reno inquired evenly, "Where is he, then?"

"That's none of your business."

Reno's voice grew hard. He said, "Sure, it's my business. My name's Jim Reno. I represent Mrs. Martin Reynolds, the owner of Sun Ranch."

"Why, old Martin," said a man who was leaning against the wall. He was a man of medium height, with fine gray eyes, gray hair, and a mustache. "How is Martin? He was always a friend of mine. I'm Mason Deevers."

Jim looked intently at Deevers and said, "He mentioned you before he died."

Deevers blinked, and the shock of the announcement went around the room. "Oh, Martin died? I didn't know about that. He was a good man." He looked at Chris and said, "You must be his son, my boy. You look just like him."

"This is Christopher Reynolds," Reno answered. "Major Reynolds died not long ago. But before he died he instructed me to bring his family out here and settle them on Sun Ranch."

Again his words ruffled the crowd, and change swept the room like a sundown's cool wind. Simon Meade glanced around at the other ranchers, then gazed back unflinchingly at Reno and Chris. "I'm sorry about Reynolds," he said, "but he let the Sun Ranch go too long. The valley only respects a man's grazing rights as long as he uses it for beef. Martin left it alone and tried to run it from too far away, and now he's got nothing to put on the grass. Other men here have got plenty of beef that are cryin' for grass. It was free range when he came here, and it's still free range today. The free range is only for the man that can show good use of it. He's no longer got the grass." He hesitated, then turned to Chris. "I'll tell you what, Mr. Reynolds. I'll buy your ground from you. Give you enough money to take your family back to Chicago."

Chris Reynolds shook his head firmly. "No, that's not what we came for. We came to make a life for ourselves out here and to build up the ranch. Thanks for the offer, though."

That Meade was not a man who liked to be crossed was evident to both Reno and Chris. He lifted his chin and his face grew flushed. "I'm sorry for your family, but that's just the way it is. You've lost the ranch, and I'd suggest you go back where you came from."

Chris gave Jim an agonized glance. Reno took a step forward, resting his hands on his gunbelt. He was thinking how trouble came constantly. Out through the windows to his right he could see the sun setting and the ragged pine crests of the hills. He was thinking that every day brings its troubles, and a man seldom has warning. Sometimes he has to give an answer on the spur of the moment and then hold to that answer until the sky falls in.

"We came a long way here from Chicago, and it'd be a longer way back." He seemed to settle, and his voice grew summer-soft as he said, "I'm taking the Reynoldses out to Sun Ranch first thing tomorrow. It's an owned ranch, and I'll expect to stay there. As long as one Sun cow walks on it, it's Sun Ranch. When there aren't any more cows, I'll turn my horse on it, and if I lose my horse, I'll stand on the grass on my own two legs and claim it."

Instantly the challenge brought fire to Simon Meade's eyes. "The moment you set foot on Sun, we'll regard you as an outlaw!"

"Regard me any way you please," Reno said just as softly as before.

"There are already plenty of outlaws on this range, and you'll just be one more of them as far as we're concerned. Is that right, men?" Meade looked around, and no one was about to stand against Meade.

No one except Mason Deevers. He spoke up instantly, "No, that's not right, Simon. We all use the free range. We cut one man out, and we're cutting our own throats."

Meade ignored Deevers and said ominously to Reno, "I'm grazing my cows on that land. If you catch one of them, to me you'll be an outlaw. Stay off Sun Ranch, and it'll be better for all concerned."

Reno stared at Meade, then his eyes ran around the room regarding the cattlemen. He seemed to be unaware of the danger that lay in the group for him. Eventually he said, "It'd be better if you shot me down here. If you let me get away from here, I'll be at Sun Ranch—" Now he stopped and looked directly at Simon Meade. "And the man that sets his dogs on me, that man I will hunt down and kill. I don't believe in trouble, but if there's going to be trouble," he ended, "I don't believe in mercy."

He turned his back on the group, said, "Come on, Chris," and left the room. They walked up the stairs and could hear the voices rising in the dining room, arguing about Jim Reno and Sun Ranch.

# SEVEN
## Sun Ranch

Lige Benoit was short, muscular, with jet-black hair and a pair of piercing dark eyes. He had been sheriff of Banning for eight years, and his reputation was such that the town was safe for the people who lived in it. Now as Benoit stepped out of his office and looked across the street, his eyes narrowed as he saw a small group emerge from Kyle Poindexter's general store. Having already heard about the Reynolds family coming to settle on Sun Ranch, he stepped off the boardwalk and strolled across the dusty street to meet the newcomers.

Benoit removed his hat to the two women and made his introduction. "I'm Lige Benoit," he said politely, then looked at Reno.

Reno answered, "Glad to know you, Sheriff. I stopped by to see you yesterday."

Benoit gave Reno careful scrutiny because out of the four, he was the one a lawman would be most interested in. He quickly analyzed Reno's smooth face, and his eyes flickered down to the .44 that hung at his side. Then, turning to the older woman, he said, "Glad to welcome you to the valley, Mrs. Reynolds."

"Thank you, Sheriff," Lillian Reynolds said. She was wearing a gray dress; her hair was done up fashionably and was topped by a small hat. She made a pretty picture as she stood there before Lige Benoit, but she appeared to be worried. "I understand there could be some trouble over our going to the ranch. Although . . ." She hesitated. "I don't understand why. After all, we do *own* the ranch."

Lige Benoit said guardedly, "I guess you've already been told that the trouble would be over the free grass sections. Quite a few of the local ranchers have been using it for graze, and nobody likes to have something taken away from him."

Ramona Reynolds spoke up. "That's certainly true, Sheriff Benoit. And we don't like to have something taken away from us."

Benoit cast a swift look at the young woman and nodded. "Yes, Miss Reynolds, I'm sure you feel that way about it. The only problem is that the ranchers seem to feel like the grass belongs to the people who are here to use it. And since your father never stayed on the place, well, the owners around here feel that he forfeited his rights."

Reno said pointedly, "I've served notice on them, Sheriff, that we'll be at Sun Ranch and waiting for anything that comes." He smiled grimly, then said, "I guess you've already heard that."

Benoit allowed himself a small smile that matched Reno's. "Yes, we've got a pretty good system of gossip around here, especially about strangers." He put his hat back on and nodded to the group, saying, "You understand that I only have authority here in town. Let me know if I can be of any help to you while you're here." He then turned and walked down the street.

"Well, that wasn't very encouraging," Chris said flatly. "What do you make of it, Jim?"

Reno shrugged and answered briefly, "We'll just have to wait and see, Chris. Let's get this stuff in the buggy, and we'll go see your new home." He and Chris loaded some supplies, picked up the luggage from the hotel, put it into the rented buggy, and left town, heading for Sun Ranch.

As they left, the banker, Dale Devaney, came out to stand beside Sheriff Benoit. He was a large, heavyset man of fifty-four with small hazel eyes and dark hair. "That looks like trouble, Sheriff," he murmured. "They can't cut it. Too many against them."

"Too bad, too bad." Benoit shrugged. "I hate it for the women and that young fella. It'd be better for them if they turned around and went back East right now. The valley'll never let them keep that grass."

★　★　★

Reno had gotten directions to Sun Ranch from the stableman. He drove the buggy south, and within two hours came to the Black River, a beautiful stream that divided the rolling grass. They passed through one valley, rose through a scented crest of pines, then entered another valley. The great row of mountains which held Bear Valley rose up around them. The river curved as it made its way across the floor of the plain, and Reno kept his eyes moving as they rode along.

The Reynoldses were quiet, intimidated by the open spaces. This venture had been merely something to talk about, but now as they crossed through the tall grass and watched the far ridges, they suddenly realized that, for better or for worse, this would be the place where they would have to survive. The sun was hot, and Reno stopped once to let the horses drink. He got down and stamped his feet, and the others followed suit.

As they stood looking across the plains, Mona murmured, "How far is it?"

"Not too far. Two hours should get us there. We'll follow the river," Reno added, "and cross over at a ford the stableman told me about."

The buggy moved along the road, raising clouds of dust, and several times they saw cattle grazing. Once as they passed through a small herd that drifted aimlessly, Reno stopped the buggy and stared at the brand.

"What's the matter?" Lillian asked, puzzled at his interest.

Reno motioned toward the cows. "See those brands? That's the Sun brand."

Lillian looked closely and saw a curve with short vertical marks over it. "Why, it does look like a rising sun," she said, pleased. "Are those our cows?"

Reno was silent for a moment, then shook his head. "They're vented, Lillian."

"Vented? What does that mean?" Chris asked with curiosity. Then he looked at the nearest cow and said, "There's another brand on them, isn't there?"

"Yes, Slash A." Reno nodded.

His words came sharply, and there was a set look on his face that made Mona ask, "Well, what does it mean, Jim?"

"It means that Slash A has taken these cows, crossed out the Sun brand, and put their own on it."

"You mean they stole them?" Chris asked with astonishment. "These cattle are rustled?"

"If Meade doesn't have a bill of sale," Reno said grimly, "that's exactly what it means." He looked all around the wide valley and pictured in his mind some of the spreads that lay encircling it. "I wouldn't be surprised if we found some of our cattle on more ranches. An absentee landlord," he explained, "is fair game for anybody."

"What will you do?" Mona asked. This was a world beyond her experience. She knew Chicago and the city, where there was a policeman just down the street and courts to try cases. But here she saw the wildness of the country and realized that there were no policemen within shouting distance. She turned to Jim, her voice troubled, and repeated, "What will you do?"

Reno turned to look at her, and there was a sudden hardness in his eyes that she had seen only once before, on the night that he had drawn his gun on the hoodlums in the streets of Chicago. "Get them back," he said laconically.

The finality of his words struck the three forcibly as they stared at him. But he continued in the same casual tone, saying, "Well, let's get home." He picked up the lines, spoke to the horses, and drove them at a fast trot on the road that paralleled the river.

Eventually the buggy crossed the river and half an hour later crested a small ridge, and Reno drew the horses up. He looked down on the scene below and waved his hand. "I think that's it," he said. Eagerly the Reynoldses looked down and were pleased with what they saw.

The house sat on the south bank of a small creek, and there were cottonwoods bunched around it. There were lodgepole corrals and a large pole-and-shake barn. The brilliant noontime sun streamed through the trees, illuminating the scene. A bunkhouse was stationed to the left of the main house, and far off through a line of trees a distant bench folded and hoisted itself hundreds of feet, forming a background for the ranch.

"Why—it's so pretty!" Mona exclaimed. She looked at the solitary white cloud that floated across the serene blue sky and the broad yellowing cottonwood leaves that fluttered gently on the trees, and was pleased with it all. "It looks like a painting from here."

Reno grinned. "Well, things always look better from a distance," he said slyly. "It'll be a little bit grubbier when we get down to it." She cast him an indignant glance, but he continued, "Don't mean to be discouraging, but you've got to remember this ranch has been without an owner for a long time. The crew's liable to be pretty rough, and the house even more so."

Lillian said unexpectedly, "It'll be all right. We can make it look pretty. Let's go see it, Jim."

Reno slapped the reins and drove down the winding road. As they approached he noticed the signs of a deteriorating ranch: fences sagging and unrepaired, the front yard littered with bottles and bits of trash, a broken window that had not been replaced. There was an air of debilitation over the whole place as he had expected. But he was pleased, on the whole, for the buildings were sound. Paint and some hard work by the crew could make a big difference.

He wheeled the buggy in close to the house, and as soon as he halted the horses, a man stepped out on the porch and stared down at them. He was a short man of about fifty with faded blue eyes, gray hair, and a short grizzled beard. He studied them thoroughly, then greeted them in a friendly fashion, "Well, howdy. You folks lost?"

Reno secured the reins, jumped to the ground, and came around to face the man. "I'm Jim Reno," he said, "and this is Mrs. Lillian Reynolds, owner of the Sun Ranch." A faint shock rose in the eyes of the older man as Jim introduced the others and then asked, "Are you here all alone?"

"Aw—yep, the boys ain't around right now." The man stepped off the porch and came to stand beside the wagon. "I'm Deacon Boone," he said. "Glad to see ya, Miz Reynolds. Your husband's not with you?"

"No," Lillian said, "my husband died recently." She saw what she thought was real regret in the eyes of the man and started to get down from the buggy. Reno moved to help her, then handed Ramona down.

"Aw, I'm right sorry to hear that, Miz Reynolds," Boone said. "Always thought well of your husband. Wished he could've been here with us more often. Well," he slapped his hand against his thigh, "you come on in and set, and I'll fix up some grub. You folks must be hungry, driving all the way out from town."

"I'll put the buggy up in the barn," Reno said. "It'll have to be taken back tomorrow." He walked away, leaving the family to go into the house, and Lillian and the others walked up onto the porch.

They were all curious about the house, which was a one-story affair that had been painted white once but now was badly in need of some attention. Stepping inside, they were all appalled by the mess they encountered. They found themselves standing in a huge room that was apparently used as kitchen, dining room, and parlor. It was cluttered with dilapidated furniture and old bits of gear cowboys might use. It looked altogether unlivable.

"I wish I'd knowed you was coming," Boone apologized. "I'd a cleaned up some of this mess." He saw the disappointment in the face of the woman. "I'm right sorry about it," he said, shrugging. "A bunch of men livin' out by themselves— well, they just give up most of their good behavior."

Lillian turned to face him and summoned up a smile, though she was dismayed by the looks of the place. "It'll be all right. I'm sure we can make it look presentable."

"Would you show us the bedrooms?" Mona asked. "I'd like to get settled down, then we can do something about this mess."

"Why, yes ma'am. You can take your choice," Boone said. He led them down a short hall, and they discovered that the bedrooms were even worse!

Mona could not keep from saying, "I've never seen such a filthy place in my life! They live like pigs!" She had spoken more sharply than she meant to, and a flush came to Deacon Boone's face.

"Yep, you're sure right about that, Miss Reynolds."

"Have the men been living in here?" Chris demanded. "I thought there was a bunkhouse out there."

"Oh, we did live out there for a while. I still do," Boone said. "But Pack and the others, they thought it'd be easier to stay in here. And since Mr. Reynolds hadn't been here in a bit—"

"Well, they'll have to move out," Mona said brusquely. "Where are they, anyway?"

"Oh, they're out working, I guess," Boone answered vaguely. "They ought to be back pretty soon. So, I'll just go out and get your luggage if you'll tell me where to put it."

All afternoon the newcomers labored, hauling junk and

gear out of the bedrooms and trying to make the house presentable. Finally Lillian looked at her hands and said with a grimace, "Look! I'm going to have blisters."

Mona's hair was lank with the heat, and the dust they had stirred up had settled on her face. She wiped at it futilely with her handkerchief and said, "I guess we're all going to have to get used to some things, Mother." She saw the disappointment on the older woman's face and went over and put her arm around her, saying as cheerfully as she could, "Don't worry. It'll look nice when we get through with it."

They worked steadily until late afternoon. Reno was just carrying a bunch of dirty clothes and old worn boots out of the house when he looked up and saw four men come riding from the river. "Here comes the crew!" he called out. "Better come out and meet them."

He stood there as the four rode up and at once identified the foreman. A man just under six feet and about thirty-five years old dismounted and crossed to stare at Reno and at the Reynoldses, who had followed him out onto the porch. "What's all this?" he growled. He was overweight, but muscular. He had muddy brown eyes and brown hair that stuck out at all angles from underneath his tall Stetson. "What're you doing in this ranch house?"

Reno said sharply, "I'm Jim Reno. I'll be running the ranch from now on." He saw shock leap into the man's eyes, and the three men who were still mounted gave startled looks at the people on the porch. "This is Mrs. Reynolds, the owner of the ranch," Reno said. "And I guess you must be Pack Ganton."

"That's me. But I don't know about all this." Ganton was a burly, aggressive man, but confronted with a situation such as this, he was uncertain. "I didn't hear anything about you coming back to the ranch."

Reno saw that Ganton was a tough one, and he met toughness with toughness. "You don't have to know anything, Ganton, except the owner's here to stay and you're back in the bunkhouse. You and the rest of you fellows." He looked at the three on the horses and asked, "What are your names?"

"I'm Ollie Dell," one of them spoke up at once. He was trim and well built, dressed better than most cowboys. He had black hair and sharp blue eyes and had the marks of a good hand. He waved at the man on his left. "This is Tuck Wilson, and this is Patch Meeks," he said, indicating the fourth member. Wilson was a man of forty with tow-colored hair and a surly look on his face. Meeks had brown eyes and brown hair. He was tall and gangly and could not meet Reno's eyes for some reason.

"All of you pile off your horses," Reno ordered, "and get your gear out of the house. Then we'll pitch in and clean up."

Pack Ganton stared at him, then looked at Lillian and said, "Let's get this straight. Am I the foreman around here or not?"

Reno knew he had to have a crew, and he had to use what was at hand. They looked like a sorry enough bunch except for Ollie Dell, but he said, "You've been foreman, and you'll stay that. Mrs. Reynolds is the owner, and I'm here to help her manage the place."

Ganton felt that he had won a victory and grinned. "Right." Then he turned to the men and said, "Put these horses up, then give Mrs. Reynolds a hand fixin' up this house." He pushed his hat back on his head, teetered back on his high-heeled boots, and ran his eyes over the family.

"Wasn't expectin' company," he said, "so the place is a mess." His eyes fell on Mona, and the startled girl felt as if he had touched her, so blatant was the way his eyes roamed over her figure. A grin came to his face, and he nodded. "Glad to have you on the ranch."

Afterwards when the men were inside cleaning up the rest of their gear, Mona moved over to stand beside Reno. Doubt was on her face as she looked up at him. "Is this the best that Dad could do? They don't look like much."

Reno glanced around the ranch house and said thought-fully, "We'll need 'em if we're going to hang onto this ranch."

"I don't like Ganton."

Reno gave her a peculiar look. "You don't have to like him. But me, I've got to do something about him." He caught her look of surprise and shrugged. "He's gotta be whipped, a man like that. You give 'im an inch, he'll take a mile."

Mona asked, "Why don't you just fire him?"

"No, he's tough, Ganton is," Reno answered, "and I'll need him. But he'll never be any good to us until he knows who's the boss. And I imagine he'll have to be taught that les-son pretty soon."

It came sooner than Reno thought. That night Boone cooked supper, and Reno said, "We better have Ganton in so we can get a report on what's been going on."

Lillian agreed, and during the meal, Pack Ganton became unbearable. When Reno attempted to ask about the condition of the ranch, Ganton sneered and said, "I'll take care of the ranch. I been doin' it for a long time now."

Reno said nothing, but Mona watched his eyes grow hooded and his lips tighten.

After the meal Ganton said, "I'll be around if you need

me. You folks don't need to worry about the cattle." He was looking at Reno as he spoke. "We don't need any amateurs tellin' us our job." He waited for Reno to speak, but there was no answer, and a smile pulled his lips apart. He turned and left the room.

As soon as he was gone a silence fell over the room, which was finally broken by Lillian. "How can we put up with a man like that?" she asked in despair.

Reno rose to his feet and said, "I'll go have a talk with him."

He left the room and walked across to the bunkhouse. Stepping inside, he saw all three of the range hands seated at a table with the foreman. Pack Ganton looked up and growled, "What you want, Reno?"

Reno said in a low voice, "Get up, Ganton." Trouble was in Reno's eyes, and his body was tense. Ganton knew it immediately, but he noted how small Reno was compared to his own bulk.

He got to his feet with a grin. "Better not try it," he said. "I'll pull your eyeballs out."

He had no time to say anything else, for without warning Reno stepped forward and delivered a powerful blow into his face. The force of it drove Ganton back against the wall, and the whole bunkhouse rattled with his fall. Ganton shook his head and reached up and touched the blood that began to flow from his nose. His eyes were clouded for a moment, then they cleared. He got to his feet stiffly, cursing.

"Why—I'll kill you!" he said and went for the gun at his hip. He never got it cleared, though, for Reno had advanced while Ganton was on the floor. He stepped forward again and delivered a roundhouse just above Ganton's belt. The force of it drew a smothered cry from Ganton, who forgot the gun and doubled up. As he fell again to the floor, Reno bent down and drew Ganton's gun out and tossed it onto the bunk.

He looked around at the other hands, who were staring with shock, then he glanced back down at Ganton. Reaching down, he pulled the big man to his feet, shoved him against the wall, and stepped back. Ganton was gasping for breath and was pale as the underside of a fish.

"You made a mistake about me, Pack," Reno said almost mildly. "From now on *I* give the orders, and *you* take 'em. That clear?"

Ganton was trying to regain his breath. After a few moments he moaned but didn't answer. Reno gave Ganton a moment to take in some air before asking coldly, "You goin' or stayin'?"

Pack Ganton took a deep breath, gritting his teeth. "I'm stayin'," he said. "I been runnin' this show a long time against stuff you don't even know about. We'll see how you do."

Reno said, "That's fine," and turned to look at the others. "What about you three? You stayin' or goin'? It's gonna be hard from here on. Your easy days are over. There's a fight shapin' up."

Ollie Dell grinned easily and looked at the other two. "We're stayin'," he said. "Never did trust a man who comes in making lots of promises." He looked directly at Reno with no fear in his eyes and said, "Interested to see how the big wind turns out."

Reno liked the spunk of the young man. "Well, we'll both find out then, won't we, Ollie?" He turned and left the room.

# EIGHT
## "He's Laying His Life on the Line"

Lula McKeever, the waitress at the Palace, glanced up and saw Simon Meade, his son, and his foreman coming through the door. Quickly she hurried over to them and gave Simon Meade a smile. "Got your usual table right over here for you, Mr. Meade."

Meade merely grunted and followed the diminutive waitress to a table over in the corner of the room and sat down heavily. "Bacon and eggs. And lots of coffee, Lula." He looked across at the other two men and nodded, "Make that three."

"Bring us some of those good biscuits, too," Lew Meade said. He grinned and winked at the waitress, which made her blush.

She murmured, "Yes, sir," and turned away.

Lew Meade at twenty-four had his father's height but was rangy rather than bulky. His red hair and dark blue eyes made him stand out—a handsome man, lean and trim. But he was not serious enough for his father. He grinned now, observing idly, "Got to take Lula out again, Dad. I been neglecting my social life lately."

Simon Meade frowned and snapped, "We've got more important things to do than run around after waitresses, Lew." He glanced over at his foreman, Bax LeFarge, studying him carefully. LeFarge was also tall, over six feet, weighing 210 pounds. He had dark brown hair and pale blue eyes, a rough man in every way, with fists and guns. He was the kind of man it took to run a big ranch like Slash A. LeFarge was not a man who talked a lot, and he sat quietly, waiting for the owner to speak.

Meade looked over the crowd, then his eyes came back to LeFarge. "Bax," he said, "we've got to do something about Sun. We need that range."

"Lots of other people think they need it too, Mr. Meade." LeFarge looked directly at his employer and added with a slight grin, "We were gonna have to fight for it, anyway. Some of these other ranchers around here have got ideas about it."

"Well, they can forget 'em!" Meade snapped abruptly. "It's closer to our range, on our side of the river, and it's a natural addition to Slash A."

Lew Meade leaned back in his chair and studied his father. He was an easygoing young man, a good cowhand when he chose to work, but he did not have the kind of driving spirit his father had. "We don't have to have it, Dad," he said easily. "We're runnin' about all the head we can handle now."

The remark angered Simon Meade. "I didn't come to this land to be a piker, Lew," he said testily. "I came to build the biggest ranch in Wyoming. And the only way we can do that is to expand south—and that means Sun. If we can get that, we'll control everything east of the river." Dissatisfaction marked his heavy face, and he said, "I don't like it, Lew, that you take this so easily. This'll be your ranch one day, and I don't want to hand over a second-rate outfit to you."

Lew Meade shrugged. "Don't see that it's worth gettin' somebody shot for, Dad. And that's what it'll come to the minute we try to move in on that grass. If not from Sun itself, it'll be from one of the valley ranchers over in the west—" He hesitated, glancing over at LeFarge, and said, "Or maybe some of Jack Bronte's men."

LeFarge gazed at Lew Meade, then nodded in agreement. "Lew may be right about that, Mr. Meade. Bronte's bunch has been using that as kind of a feeder ground. They take those cattle of Sun's, run 'em up into the pocket, and sell 'em off." His face grew cloudy as he said, "They been gettin' some of our stock, too. I think it's time to take our crew up and wipe Bronte and his hard cases out."

Meade nodded sharply. "All in good time. We'll take care of this Sun business, and then we'll take care of Jack Bronte." He thought a moment, then said, "This fellow Reno. He seems like a hard one. And I don't like what he's been doing out at Sun for the past week. You'll have to be ready for him, Bax. Take care of it."

"All right." LeFarge was accustomed to such orders, having cleared the Slash A range of everyone who had tried to put down roots there in the last five years. Jim Reno was just another obstacle to be removed so Slash A could continue to grow.

"Hey, look," Lew said suddenly, "there's Dave Holly." A grin touched his wide lips and he said, "Reckon he's come to town to see that new woman of his. And she's somethin' to see, I can tell you!"

Simon Meade lifted his eyes and followed Holly's sturdy figure. He waited until the man ascended the hotel stairs, then shook his head and snorted in disgust. "A man's a fool to get a wife through the mails. I thought Holly had more sense."

The object of their conversation slowed down as he approached the top of the stairs, and as he walked down the hall his steps grew even slower. This was unusual for Holly, for he was ordinarily a man who ran head-on at everything with all of his strength, but the determination that was such a part of him had somehow faltered in his dealings with Belle Montez. Ever since she'd come to town and he'd set eyes on her, he had been confused. He was drawn to her dark beauty, yet something in him refused to make the final decision to marry her. He hated the lack of resolution. As he got to her door and knocked on it he thought, *I've got to make up my mind one way or the other. It can't go on like this.*

The door opened, and he swept his hat off, saying, "Good morning, Belle. Are you ready?"

"Yes." Belle was wearing a sky-blue dress nipped tightly at the waist and a small blue hat. She stepped out, taking Holly's arm, and as the two of them walked down the hall she smiled at him warmly. "I'm anxious to see the ranch," she said.

Holly shrugged as they started down the stairs. "Well, it's not fancy, but I'm proud of it."

He led her down the stairs and out of the hotel into the hot sunshine. He handed her up into the buggy, climbed in beside her, and they left Banning at a brisk pace. As they drove along he noted that she took in all the details of their ride. It was a good ranch. Holly had worked hard to build it from nothing and for some years had thought of nothing but making it grow. But the loneliness of his life had become unbearable, and he'd somehow been too awkward to find a wife among the few young women in the valley. He was angry now at his inability to please a woman with light talk, and he grew diffident.

"Well, it's not a woman's place, Belle," he said quickly,

helping her down as they arrived, "but it's a good ranch." He introduced her to his cook, a half-breed Indian woman named Daisy, who was married to one of his hands, and then showed her around the house.

Belle was amused, at first, at Holly's anxiety. She went through the house and could honestly appreciate the sturdiness of it, though it had none of the amenities a woman would put in it. After she saw the house he led her outside. They walked around the corrals, and he showed her the creek that watered the stock.

As they walked back toward the house, he said slowly, "It's just a small-time ranch, Belle. It'll never be like Slash A or the Oxbow. The room's all taken in this valley. No place to spread to."

A thought occurred to Belle and she asked, "Is that what the trouble's about? The people I came in with on the stage?"

"Yeah, the Reynolds place." Holly nodded. "They're gonna have trouble. That Simon Meade is a pretty tough old bird. He'll never be satisfied till he owns all the grazing land east of the river."

"But he doesn't own it, does he?"

"No, it's free range right now, except for the small section Sun Ranch sits on. But that don't mean anything around here."

"Would you take that land yourself, Dave?" Belle asked curiously, turning her dark eyes on him.

Holly was disturbed by her question. The truth was, he had planned to use some of the grazing land himself if Slash A continued to put the pressure on Sun. But he knew he could never explain such a thing to Belle. "I won't have to decide right now, I guess." He shrugged. "I guess it looks pretty wrong to a newcomer like you."

Belle saw he was troubled by his thoughts and said no more.

The visit lasted only a couple of hours, then Holly took Belle to the buggy and started back for town. As they moved along, he watched the clouds and noted the dust raised by some rider across the plains. He talked about the ranch and what he hoped to do with it, but he said nothing about the two of them. Desperately he had wrestled with their situation, but he could not bring himself to ask Belle to marry him. Something inside him rose up like a wall, choking off his words.

Belle waited all the way back to town for him to mention marriage, but being an astute young woman, she saw that he had no intention of doing so. Once back at the hotel, Dave escorted her back up to her room, stopping at the door. Hesitantly he said, "Well, that's the ranch." He stumbled over his words, saying, "I—I think you ought to wait a little longer before making your mind up, Belle. It's a big decision for a woman to make." He felt her dark eyes intense on his face, and he flushed, knowing he was making a bad job of it. "Let's wait another week. We can, well, get to know each other better, and then we can talk about it."

"All right, Dave, if that's what you want. It was a nice trip, and I like your ranch very much."

She turned and entered her room, and when the door shut Holly stood staring at it. He was angry at himself and turned and walked down the stairs heavily. *What's the matter with me?* his mind yelled. *She's more than I ever thought I'd get—what am I waiting for?* Some tiny voice inside him whispered, *The bargain looks too good. How do I know she can leave her past life behind her?* For deep in Dave Holly ran a suspicious streak. He'd had to work for everything he ever got, and to be suddenly handed a woman like this seemed dangerous, though he could not have told how. He left the hotel and rode out of town angry and uncertain with himself.

From her window Belle watched him leave, and a sadness filled her heart. She had to be strong to make her way in a man's world and had been hurt often enough. The sight of Dave Holly riding out of town somehow brought home to her all that was lacking in her life—a husband, children, a home. She leaned her head against the window frame and shut her eyes, fighting off the tears that came suddenly, unexpectedly, and she remained there, silent, for a long time.

★ ★ ★

Mona Reynolds lay for a moment in the dust of the corral, stunned and almost unaware of where she was. Then she struggled to her hands and knees and glared balefully at the little bay mare that seemed to be staring at her with a malevolent expression. "You ornery thing!" she growled between her teeth and got to her feet, ignoring the pain. As she hobbled over to the corral fence, she opened the gate and stalked toward the ranch house.

She was startled when a voice said, "That was a pretty rough fall."

Mona whirled and saw that Jim Reno had appeared and was watching her carefully. A flush came to her face, and a streak of anger shot through her. "Don't you have anything to do but stand around watching me trying to ride that fool horse!" she demanded. Her hair had been shaken loose and hung over her shoulders; she made a rather pathetic picture as she stood stiffly before him. She was aware of this, which made her even more angry. "What did you do? Pick the worst horse on the ranch for me to ride?"

Reno cocked his head and tilted his hat back with a slow, deliberate movement. He was aware that Mona had been having a difficult time with the mare, and he had offered to help. But she had frozen him out with the single statement: "I suppose I know how to ride a horse without your help."

That may have been true, but the horses she had ridden at the riding stable in Chicago did not have the spirit of Ruby, the little horse Jim had picked out for her. Ruby was lively enough, and he regretted now that he hadn't picked a more sedate mount. "Well," he said apologetically, "I'll find you another horse. That one is a bit of a handful, I suppose." He hesitated, then added in the way of an apology, "The more spirited the horse, the better the mount it is, so I thought if you two could learn to get along—"

"Never mind. I'll keep this one," Mona snapped. She turned and started to the house, then whirled and burst out, "I want to warn you that I won't stand for what you've been doing to Chris! What are you trying to do, kill him?"

"I don't know what you mean."

"I mean having him strap on a gun and putting him on outlaw horses and making him ride until dark! He's not used to such things!"

"No, he's not," Reno admitted. "But if he's going to stay out here, Mona, he's going to have to get used to it. It's a tough world, and to tell the truth, I've been pretty proud of Chris. He's come a long way. Took a lot of falls and hasn't complained a single time."

"And *I* have—is that what you're trying to say?"

Everything that Reno did seemed to irritate Mona Reynolds. Once she had admitted to herself that it was because she found him attractive, but she could not imagine herself ever

falling in love with a man who was so domineering. Still, she
still found herself thinking of him. But now standing there,
watching him as he looked at her impassively, she felt her
cheeks glowing, knowing she was in the wrong. She had
talked with her mother, and even Lillian had commended
Chris for his adaptation to ranch life. Lillian herself had done
better at giving up the comfort of Chicago and a fine house
and servants than had Mona. Lillian had become the pupil of
Deacon Boone and had learned to cook such exotic specialties
as son-of-a-gun stew and, what's more, had appeared to like it.

But Mona had been resistant. She had not gotten over
her anger at her father for having caused such a difficult life
for her family, although she had said nothing to anyone. But
she had taken it out on Reno and did so now as he stood there
watching her. "I might as well tell you," she said, "I think
you're going about this whole thing wrong."

"What thing is that, Mona?"

"This business of building the ranch up here. I've heard
you talk to some of the ranchers, and you're doing nothing but
making enemies for us. The thing to do is to work it out peaceably. Get everyone around a table and talk about it like civilized
people."

Reno lifted one eyebrow. "Didn't Chris tell you what went
on when I talked to the owners?"

"Yes, he told me," Mona said reluctantly. "But perhaps
you're not the one to talk to them. You're so—so—" she hesitated, then let out an exasperated breath. "So demanding!
What we need is a moderator here! Perhaps I could do better."

Reno smiled, but crossed his arms in a firm gesture. "You
don't know this country, Mona. These are the most greedy
men you ever saw. They might be nice and take off their hats

when you come into the room, but when the cattle get hungry in the dry part of summer, they're going to move them onto this grass. They've been using it for a long time, and they'll do it again."

"Well, I don't agree. And I demand to go with you the next time you have a meeting with any of them."

"Be glad to have you. We're going over to pick up some of our stock pretty soon from Simon Meade." A streak of humor ran through him, lifting the corners of his lips, and he stood there, making an idle shape in the morning sunshine. There was a looseness about him and at the same time a tension that Mona could never understand. He was like a cat—sleepy most of the time, with his eyes half-hooded, and yet she had seen him explode into action when the need came. "Better bring your gun along, though. Don't think Meade's gonna surrender those cattle peaceably."

Mona stared at him, trying to comprehend the idea, and finally put her hands on her hips. "We can't go over with guns to take the man's cows away," she said firmly.

"*Our* cows," Reno remarked briefly.

"Then we'll have to get the law to do it."

"We'll have to import it from Cheyenne, then, 'cause there are no federal marshals out here. And the sheriff in town's not going to help us," he tried to explain again. He had hinted before at what a difficult task it would be, and now his voice hardened a little. "Look, Mona, the job your father left us is going to be tough enough. We're going to have enough people to fight without fighting each other. I'll tell you right now—if Sun survives, it'll be because it stands on its hind legs and claims what belongs to it! Now, the quicker you get that in your head, the better."

Mona's eyes grew stormy. She was not accustomed to being spoken to in such a manner, and without a word she turned and stalked toward the house. When she got inside she found her mother in the middle of a project with Deacon Boone, the two of them standing at a table covered with cooking ingredients.

"Hello, dear. Did you have a nice ride?" Lillian asked pleasantly.

"No! I mean, it was all right," Mona covered quickly. Then she plunged right in, ignoring Boone. "Mother, did you know that Jim's going to go over with the crew and take a bunch of cows away from Simon Meade this week?"

"Yes, Jim mentioned that he might do that," Lillian said. She looked up at her daughter and saw the anger in her eyes. "What's the matter, dear?"

"That's stealing! It's rustling! That's what they call it out here, isn't it, Deacon?"

Boone's faded blue eyes searched Mona's angry face, and he gestured with a gnarled hand. "Way I look at it around here, Meade stole those cows from Sun. He's the rustler, not us!"

"But he's an important rancher! The biggest in the valley!" Mona argued.

"Then that makes him the biggest rustler, I reckon," Deacon said simply. He picked up an onion and began to peel it thoughtfully. "You know, Miss Mona, we'd all like to see peace. That's what the Lord intends for the whole earth. But looks like till Jesus comes back again, God's people have to put up a fight from time to time. And speakin' personal, I'm glad Jim Reno showed up." He paused, then looked up at the two women, adding, "I might as well tell you this. If he hadn't come, you wouldn't be at this here ranch right now. The only reason Meade's hangin' back is 'cause of Jim. He's put some fire into this crew, and Meade knows he'll have to fight for it."

"We didn't come out here to get involved in a war!" Mona protested.

"I know you didn't, but it looks like that's the way it's gonna have to be, Miss Mona. And I'm of the opinion that a man oughta take his spurs off when he's talkin' to Jim. He doesn't like the idea of a fight anymore 'n you do, but he's doin' it 'cause he made a promise to your dad. And I think he'd be right proud of Jim if he was here to see what was goin' on."

Lillian did not like arguments, but she had been over this in her mind many times. Her brief time on the ranch had changed her thinking, and she had looked back to see that part of the responsibility for their position rested on her shoulders. She had thought about how she had spent money lavishly, demanding more and more, and had in reality pushed Martin into doing chancy things with finances in order to satisfy her frivolous wants. She had not spoken of this to the children, but the reality of the situation was clear and strong in her. Now she saw that the only way she could make any restitution to the memory of her husband—and to the children—was to see that Sun Ranch became a good place, a place for the family to take hold and grow. Now she said firmly, "Deacon is right, Mona. I've seen how you treat Jim, and I wish you'd think about it a little bit. He's a good man, and he's laying his life on the line for us."

Mona stared at her mother, speechless. Lillian Reynolds had never been a woman to take any role in the affairs of the family, always following the lead of her husband. Mona herself had been the one who furnished what leadership there was, other than that of her father. She disagreed violently but saw that it would be useless to argue. She said vehemently, "Well, I think he's wrong, and I think he's going to lead us into a lot of trouble." She whirled and left the kitchen, indignation evident in the straight set of her back.

"I'm worried about her, Deacon," Lillian murmured. "She's always been headstrong, even as a child." She looked up at him and added, "It was my fault. I spoiled her."

"Well, we can't go back, can we now, Miss Lillian? The good Lord, he's able to change things. He can change Miss Mona, and he can give us this ranch. And Mr. Martin now, he'll know all about that up in heaven. And he'll be saying, 'Hallelujah!'"

Lillian's eyes crinkled as she smiled and asked, "You're certain of that? That people in heaven know what we're doing on earth?"

"Why, shore I am! It prob'ly says so somewheres in the Bible, but I just ain't got to that part yet!"

Lillian laughed and said, "Let's get this stew made. Those men are going to come in hungry tonight."

# NINE
## A Trip to Town

The instant Reno turned his horse down the main street of Banning, he felt the turbulence of the town. He had been in towns like this before, where one faction had been pitted against another, and there was a tightness in the air that one did not find in places where there was no trouble. Passing along the street, he noticed four men standing outside the Lady Rose Saloon. One of them drew his eyes, and he saw that it was the same man he had put off the stage—Lester Box—and his senses sharpened. He was aware that the four men were staring at him carefully as he rode past, but he gave them only a glance, then led the buckskin down the street to the post office. Dismounting and tying his horse, he walked inside and was surprised to find Belle Montez there. Pulling his hat off he walked up beside her and smiled. "Hello, Belle," he said. "Good to see you again."

"Jim!" Belle instantly warmed to him and smiled. "How have you been? I haven't seen you around lately."

"All right," he replied. "Lots of work out at the ranch." At that moment the clerk came to stand before him, and Reno reached into his pocket and handed him a letter. "I'd like to mail this."

The clerk, a tall, thin man with thick glasses, peered at it, then grunted, "That'll be two cents."

Jim fished in his pocket, found a couple of copper coins, and passed them to the clerk. Turning to Belle, he said, "How about something cool to drink? Some lemonade or something like that, maybe?"

Belle at once said, "Fine, we can go back to the hotel. They got some fresh lemons in yesterday. It'll be wet, but not cool."

They stepped outside, and as they started down the street toward the hotel, Reno asked idly, "When's the wedding?" Immediately he was aware he had said the wrong thing. Belle's face tightened, her lips making a sharp line across her face. *When am I gonna learn to keep my mouth shut?* he thought, angry at himself. He could think of no way, however, to unsay the question nor any way to make it seem less impertinent.

Belle glanced at him out of the corner of her eyes and said quietly, "He doesn't want me, Jim."

Surprise came to Reno then for he had expected the marriage to be in the near future if it had not already taken place. He said shortly, "Holly's a fool."

Belle Montez smiled suddenly, and he saw that at last he had said something right. There was a tension and a tightness in her that he now had an answer for; she was a woman rejected. He couldn't understand why. She made a dismissing gesture with one graceful hand and said, "Oh, Dave's no fool, but thank you anyway. He just doesn't want me, that's all."

"Well, what does he want?" Jim demanded, almost explosively.

"He wants a plain woman," Belle answered tightly. "You know what he means by that?" She turned to look at him fully, stopping on the street, unaware of the other people passing on the sidewalk. "He means a good woman."

Reno now understood the whole situation. The pain that etched her eyes was clear and belied her casual tone. He had known from his first glance at Belle Montez that she was a woman of experience. There was a slight veneer of hardness about her that he knew had come through harsh experience in a tough world. She had been, he guessed, sought after by many men, but none of them had brought her what it was she wanted most.

He said quietly, "I'm sorry, Belle. And I still think Holly's a fool."

Belle continued to stare at him intensely. "What would you have done, Jim, if I'd come to you that first day?"

"I would've married you by now," he said, nodding firmly.

She put her hand on his arm and turned, and they continued their walk. "Thank you, Jim," she whispered. "I needed someone to say that. I never told you, but there was a bargain between us—Holly and me. He needed a wife, I needed a home, and I thought it would all work out."

Reno wanted to say something that would wipe the doubt out of her eyes. "Somewhere there's a man for you, Belle, and for him you'll have everything."

Belle smiled briefly, then shrugged her shoulders. "But I'm telling you all my troubles." She glanced down the sidewalk to where the four men were standing in a group and lowered her voice. "Things are bad, Jim. I hear talk. They're not going to let you be at peace out at Sun Ranch."

"No, they won't."

"Fight them!" she said. The fierceness of her reply startled him, and he glanced at her. She narrowed her eyes and said, "Trust no one!"

He looked at the strain on her dark face and heard the deep-seated bitterness in her voice. "Somebody's left his hoof marks all over you. Listen, you can't live without trusting someone."

"You'll be hurt if you try it."

"Everybody gets hurt. But you can't hide in a black cave and live small."

She hesitated, then looked at him. "You know why I can't believe in people. You've always known."

"I know," he said quietly. "I know something else, too. There's more to you than that. There's something good in you."

The pressure of her fingers grew quite strong on his arm. Her voice changed and was filled with emotion. "There is," she whispered. "There's so much more. But what good is that now?"

"You came out here to start over, didn't you?"

"I did, but it won't work. You saw what I was, and so did Dave. It's no use."

"Holly," said Reno harshly, "needs to open his eyes and take another look." He would have said more, but they had come abreast of the four cowboys. Alarm ran along his nerves as the tall, lean man he had put off the stage suddenly stepped out in front of them, blocking their way. The man's eyes were fixed defiantly on Reno, and there was heavy tension in the air.

"You're the yahoo that put me off the stage," Box said threateningly. "No man can do that to me! I'm gonna teach you better manners."

Reno stared at him, then nodded. "Sure. Just let this lady go on, then we can take it up."

Box leered at Belle, saying, "Lady? That ain't no lady. You ain't been around good company enough to know a lady when you see one, Reno. She ain't nothin' but a tramp!"

"Go on, Belle," Jim said in a low voice and gave her a slight nudge. She looked at him with fear in her eyes and started to speak, but he stopped her. "Go on now, this'll be all right. Go back to the hotel."

As Belle moved away, Reno said, "Look. If it's a fight you want, you can—"

He didn't complete his sentence because a blow came crashing to his head and drove him to the sidewalk. He knew faintly that he had been struck by one of the men who had come up behind him. For a moment he couldn't move, but then as he struggled to come to his feet, a pain caught him violently in the side as Box kicked him with his sharp-toed boot. He heard Box say, "I'm gonna bust you up, Reno. You ain't kicking nobody else off the stage. Hold 'im up."

He felt his arms being seized, and he tried to pull away, but the men were too strong for him. He opened his eyes and saw the face of Lester Box, his eyes gleaming, then was caught flush in the mouth with a hard right from the tall man. He felt his lips crush against his teeth, and he tasted the sharp tang of blood. He tried to get away, but the blows kept coming, one striking him on the side and bringing pain such as he'd never felt before. Consciousness began to fade away, and he slumped helplessly into the arms of the other men.

Box was still raining blow after blow on Reno's helpless face when a voice rang out coldly, "Stop right there!"

Box turned to look and saw that Belle had drawn a pepper-box from her purse—one of those short, deadly revolvers used by gamblers, accurate for no more than ten feet, but powerful. He stared down not one, but six barrels as she pointed the gun at his head. Box held his hands up and said hastily, "Now wait a minute—"

"You scum! I think I'll just shoot you now!" Belle said, her voice low and intense, her hand steady. Then Belle said, "Get away from him!" When he didn't move, her finger tightened on the trigger.

"Wait a minute! Wait!" he gasped.

At that moment another voice rang out, "What's going on here?" Sheriff Lige Benoit appeared, his black eyes fixed on the men. He had drawn his gun and now held it on the other three men, saying, "The fun's over. All of you are going to the pokey." When they started to protest, he waved his gun and said, "Shut up!" He looked more closely at Reno and said, "He's gonna need the doctor, but he's gone to deliver a baby over at the Jenkins place."

Belle slipped the gun back into her purse and said firmly, "Have him taken up to my room. I'll clean him up, and the doctor can see him when he gets back."

Benoit cast her a curious look, then nodded, saying, "You two get him up there. Box, you and Pounders come with me."

Belle led the two men to the hotel. They had to carry Reno, who had passed out. As they left, Box said, "You're not gonna get away with this, Sheriff—"

"You shut your mouth 'fore I ram this muzzle down your gullet!" Benoit snapped. "I know your boss'll get you out, but you're going to enjoy the hospitality of the town and pay a fine." When the other two men exited the hotel, Benoit barked, "Now git movin'!" and herded the men down to the jail. As he walked he thought, *That was a pretty bad beating Reno took. A lot of men can't come back after a thing like that.*

★  ★  ★

Consciousness came back to Reno in the form of a sharp, stabbing pain in his side as he took a deep breath, and the feeling of something cold and wet on his face. There was a roaring in his ears, and he couldn't think for a moment. Finally he opened his eyes and saw Belle Montez bending over him, the memory of the beating coming back to him.

"Don't move, Jim," Belle said gently. "The doctor thinks you might have some cracked ribs."

Reno blinked his eyes and took a deep breath that sent another pain through him. "Doctor?"

"Yes, about an hour ago. You slept right through it. See, he tied your ribs up tight and put the bandages on your chest."

Reno glanced down to see that his shirt was off, and his chest was bound with roll after roll of white bandages. "Funny," he said, "I don't even remember his being here."

"You were lucky. The doctor was out delivering a baby, but the birth was easy, and he got back to town before he expected to. Otherwise, you'd still be a mess." Belle continued to bathe his face with a cool cloth. "Your face is pretty bad, too. But the swelling will go down after a while."

Reno made a futile attempt to get up, saying, "I can't stay here! This is your room, isn't it?"

"Yes, but you have to stay here. You're not able to ride a horse." She paused and then put her hand on his forehead. "It'll be all right."

"No, it won't. It won't look good to the town, you having a man in your room."

Her lips grew firm, and she said stubbornly, "Let the town think what it will. You need care, and I'm going to see to it that you get it."

A wave of nausea washed over Reno then, and he lay back, shutting his eyes. "Hate to be a bother," he whispered. He managed a weak smile and then said so softly that Belle barely heard him, "Some birthday," and then drifted off again.

Belle saw that he was unconscious and slowly put her hand on his crisp black hair. Then, struck by an impulse she could not resist, she bent over and kissed his forehead. Her lips remained there for a moment, then she whispered softly, "You're not a bother. And happy birthday, Jim."

★  ★  ★

When Reno did not return to the ranch by dark, Lillian began to get worried. "I don't know why he's taking so long," she said fretfully to Mona. "He only had to pick up a few things."

Mona shrugged, saying, "He probably stayed in town to catch up on his drinking and gambling." She had no idea if this were true or not, but she was still upset with Reno and their whole situation.

But the next morning when he still had not come in, she, too, began to be worried. As the three of them were finishing breakfast, Chris said, "I think I'd better ride in and check up on Jim. It's not like him to stay away like this."

But before he got up from the table, there was the sound of a horse approaching. Chris looked out the window. "I wonder who that is? I don't know him."

He walked to the front door and stepped outside. Mona curiously followed him and saw that the man was tall, a little over six feet, with red hair. He got down from his horse and, seeing Mona, removed his hat. "Hello," he said with a slight smile. "My name's Lew Meade. I guess you folks would be the Reynoldses."

Lillian had come out onto the porch, too, and she said, "Yes, I'm Lillian Reynolds. This is my son, Chris, and my daughter, Ramona. Won't you come in, Mr. Meade?"

"That's a kind thought," he said, "but I'm going into town." He hesitated, then asked, "Did you hear about what happened to Jim Reno?"

"What is it?" Lillian demanded quickly.

Meade looked down at his boots, not knowing quite how to frame a reply, then looked back up and shrugged. "I really don't know much about it, but some of the boys got in last night from town. There was some kind of trouble over a woman there, and Reno got hurt. Didn't know whether you'd heard about it or not, so I thought I'd stop in and let you know."

"We'll have to go in," Chris said immediately. "I'll get the wagon so we can bring him home."

When Chris went to hitch up the wagon, Mona said, "Did you hear how bad he was hurt, or who the woman was?"

"I don't think it's fatal. And the woman was the one that Dave Holly brought in to marry. She must be something," Meade said with an admiring grin. "Way I hear it, Reno was getting the worst of the fight, and she pulled a pistol out of her purse and stopped our boys." He laughed outright then, saying, "I never saw men so mad as our fellas were! Gettin' run off by a woman! They even got thrown in jail and fined."

"You don't seem to be too angry about it," Lillian observed. "Aren't you upset that some of your men were humiliated?"

Lew Meade's grin grew even broader. "Aw, those fellas

deserve it. Besides, you can never count on what a woman'll do." His eyes fell on Mona, and he went on, "No insult intended, Miss Ramona. Well, I'll be going." He looked around the spread and said more soberly, "Been meaning to get over, but just hadn't made it yet."

"Your father doesn't feel so friendly," Mona said tartly. "He's pretty much told us to get out of here."

Lew Meade searched her face. He stared at Mona for a moment, then said soberly, "Truth is, I don't agree with my father about all of this. We've got enough land where we are. I've tried to tell him, but somehow he's got a disease, always wanting more." He replaced his hat and mounted his horse. "I'm sorry for any trouble you've been put to. I'll try to talk some sense into him. And if I can ever help you, you folks let me know." He pulled on the brim of his hat as a final courtesy, wheeled his horse around, and rode off.

"That seems to be a fine young man," Lillian observed. "Not at all like what I hear his father is." The two of them stood there speaking quietly until Chris drove the wagon around.

Mona said, "Chris, you've got to stay and go with the hands. Someone's got to be with them. I'll go bring Jim back."

Chris argued, but he knew she was right. Mona went inside, got her hat, and came back out, getting into the wagon. "I don't know when I'll be back," she said. "If he's not able to travel, I'll have to stay over in the hotel and wait until tomorrow." She bid them good-bye, then drove the wagon out of the yard.

All the way into town she thought about what Lew Meade had said. Somehow it didn't sound like Reno, but then what did she know about him? He was handsome enough, certainly a man that women would look at, but it offended her that the man in charge of their ranch would get into a brawl over a woman.

She pulled up in front of the Palace, went inside, and stopped at the desk.

"Yes, ma'am, can I help you?" the clerk asked.

"I'd like to see—" She paused suddenly because she didn't know the woman's name. So she said rather lamely, "Is Jim Reno here?"

A grin touched the lips of the clerk, and he nodded. "Yes, ma'am, he's in Miss Montez's room. That'll be room 206."

"Thank you," Mona said stiffly. She knew the clerk was laughing at her, and her cheeks turned red.

As she turned toward the stairs, a man was about to go up. He gave her a quick look, then pulled his hat off. "You must be Miss Reynolds," he said. "I saw you when you came in on the stage. I'm Dave Holly."

Mona looked at him, a little startled, not expecting to meet him. She noted the worry in his hazel eyes and the nervousness that made him fidget with the hat in his hands. "How are you, Mr. Holly?" she said. "I just got into town. We didn't hear what happened until this morning. What do you know about it?"

Holly shook his head. There was a line of bitterness that scored his mouth as he answered, "Not a thing. I got word this morning, too." He stood there awkwardly, looking down at the floor for a moment, then lifted his eyes to meet hers. "It's bad. I wish it hadn't happened." Then he asked, "Do you know anything about this man Reno?"

"He's helping us get the ranch put together, as you know," Mona answered. She wanted to ask about the woman but felt that it would be out of place. So instead she said, "Perhaps we'd better go up and see what really happened."

At his gesture she ascended the stairs, and when they got to the room, she knocked lightly. There was a slight bustle inside, then the door opened. She was met by a woman in her late twenties with very dark hair and eyes. "Hello, Belle," Holly said over Mona's shoulder. "This is Miss Ramona Reynolds. She came to see about Reno."

Mona said, a little disconcerted, "Oh, of course, we've met. We came in on the stage together." She hadn't connected Belle Montez with Dave Holly until now.

Holly said shortly, "Oh, that's right. What about Reno?"

The tone of his voice brought a strange expression to Belle Montez's face. She knew men, and she saw at once that Holly was angry. "Come in," she said.

They entered and saw that the single bed in the room was empty and had been made up. This threw Holly off stride, and he stood there, trying to figure out how to ask the question, but Mona beat him to it.

"We heard that Reno was hurt," she said.

"Yes, he was badly beaten," Belle answered, nodding. "The doctor was out of town yesterday afternoon, so I had him brought here until he could be seen to."

"Well, where is he now?" Mona demanded impatiently.

"He wouldn't stay here. He had a bad night last night after the doctor saw him, but this morning he crawled out of bed and said he'd make it by himself. He's in the room next door."

Mona said crisply, "Thank you." Her voice was cold as she turned and left the room.

As soon as the door shut, Holly blurted out, "What did you do a thing like that for, bringing him to your room, Belle? Didn't you know how it would look?"

"He was hurt, Dave. And the doctor wasn't in town."

"Well . . . did he stay here all night?"

"Yes."

The bare syllable and the look in Belle's eyes confused Holly. He was a straightforward man, liking things to go evenly and disliking complications. But now he was right in the middle of one. He wanted to rail at the woman, to preach at her, but managed to fight down the impulse. He stood watching her, and an idea began to grow in his mind, one that he didn't like. He didn't know how to get around it. It had come to him that Belle was more interested in Jim Reno than she should be. He sighed deeply then and said, "This isn't the way I wanted it to be, Belle. I don't like it."

"I'm sorry, but I had to do it," Belle said quietly. "He was helpless, and I'm the whole reason those men had it in for him in the first place. I had to do something."

"Well, I guess it's all right then. No damage done." He made the observation and saw that it angered Belle.

"No damage done? Why, they would have killed him if I hadn't been there, Dave! And things aren't going to get any easier for him! He's going to get killed, sure enough, if he tries to fight the battles for the Reynoldses!" She was angry clear through, first at Dave for his suspicions, which she read clearly, then at the Reynolds family for using Reno. She didn't really know anything about the Reynoldses, except that she had seen the heartlessness of Ramona, and she suspected that the rest of the family was no better. "I'm tired, Dave. I want to lie down and rest a while."

Holly knew he was being dismissed and tried to soften his manner. "Sorry if I seemed abrupt, Belle," he said, "but I heard about this and didn't know what was going on. Could I come back later, and we'll have lunch together?"

"If you like." Her reply was brief, and he turned at once and left the room. He was angry, mostly at himself for handling the matter badly. Seemed like nothing he had done had been right since Belle had come to town, and he grew moody and irritable as he went down the stairs and left the hotel.

When Mona left Belle's room she knocked on the next door down the hall and heard a voice say, "Come in." She opened it and found Jim Reno lying full length on the bed. His boots were off, but he was fully dressed. He looked at her and nodded. "Come on in." He drew himself up painfully into a sitting position. His face was puffy, and she could see he had taken a bad beating. "Sit down, Mona," he said.

Mona shook her head. "No, I won't stay. I just heard about the fight this morning." She hesitated, then said, "We were worried." The sight of his bruised face and the obvious pain he was in drove away most of the anger she had felt. She asked, "Are you badly hurt?"

He grinned at her crookedly. "Well, I been stomped worse. I'll be OK."

"What happened, Jim?"

She listened as he briefly related the incident and ended by saying, "It's a good thing Belle was there. I don't think I'd have a whole bone left in my body if those fellas had time to finish what they started."

"I'm glad she was there." She clasped her hands together and said suddenly, "It wouldn't have done any good for me to be there. I don't carry a gun." Even to her own ears it sounded like a slur, and she hastened to add, "It's a good thing she does. I brought the wagon, Jim. We can fix a bed in the back if you're ready to go back to the ranch."

"I guess so. No sense running up a bill around here. You

can bring the wagon around, and I'll get myself pulled together. We'll get my horse at the livery and hitch him to the wagon. Then we can go."

"All right." She half turned toward the door, wanting to say something to atone for the anger that she had felt. She saw him struggling to get up and simply said, "I'll go get the wagon." As she went down the stairs she thought, *I'll have to be more kind to him.*

# TEN
## *Slash A Takes a Fall*

Two weeks after the fight in Banning, Jim unexpectedly appeared on Monday morning at the bunkhouse. The crew looked up in surprise when he said, "Everybody get mounted. We're gonna make a visit." Something in his voice seemed different. He had said little since the affair in town, and the crew had wondered if he was going to be the same again.

Now Ganton stared at him, asking, "Where are we goin'? We got that bunch to move over on the south pasture." He was resentful at having to take Reno's orders and rarely heard one without questioning it.

Reno looked at Ganton, then the rest of the men, and said briefly, "Bring your guns. There's liable to be some trouble." He saw that his remarks had brightened the eyes of Ollie Dell, who grinned at him recklessly. Dell was a small young man, but feisty and ready for trouble at all times. Tuck Wilson and Patch Meeks, on the other hand, looked disgruntled, but rose to their feet and followed Reno outside.

They said nothing, but mounted and left the ranch, Reno leading them in a northerly direction. He did not put them in a driving pace, so they rode in a small bunch, close enough to speak to one another. Finally Ganton couldn't stand it any longer. "What's this all about, Reno? We don't have anything up north here."

"You don't think so? Some of our cattle are up there, Ganton. We're going to collect them."

Ganton shut his mouth then, and they rode along silently for a while. Then he turned in the saddle back to Reno and asked, "You're not talking about Slash A and those vented cattle, are you?"

"That's it. We're gonna bring 'em home again."

"Why, you're crazy!" Ganton burst out, eyes wild with shock. "Old man Meade's got thirty hands there! They'd shoot us to ribbons if we tried a thing like that! Or stretch our necks from a tree!"

Reno knew that the other hands were listening, and he decided it was time to settle the matter between him and Ganton. "I heard you were tough, Pack," he sneered, his dark eyes looking him up and down. "But it doesn't sound like that to me." He looked back at the others, saying, "You boys have had a pretty easy thing here. But I think the valley's got your number. You don't have any backbone."

"We'll see about that!" Ollie Dell spoke up. He was wearing a gray outfit and a pair of fancy tooled boots. His hat was low crowned and had a snakeskin band.

Reno studied him, thinking he might be just a dresser, but something in the younger man's eyes made him smile. "OK, Ollie. It may just be you and me."

The remark went against the grain for Wilson and Meeks. Wilson said, "We'll all go." He was sullen, but there was a toughness in the man.

Patch Meeks, tall and gangly, nodded. "Yeah. We'll go, and we'll prob'ly all get shot for it."

Reno could hope for no more, and he headed north at the same steady pace. When Dell drifted close to him, Reno asked quietly, "You like to fight, Ollie?"

"Jim, I'll fight anything, anywhere. The bigger the jag, the better I like it. If you're promising some fun, that's fine." Then he gave Reno a challenging look. "If you don't deliver the fun, maybe I'll take it out of you."

The sun was round in the east, directly above the hills, and the air was crisp and clean that early morning. The great mountains in the west looked very near. As they rode, Reno studied the crew. He knew very little about them. Pack would sell him out, he was sure of that. Wilson and Meeks would fight if they had to. But only Ollie Dell had real sand.

They came to the river that separated the two ranches, the surface sparkling in the fresh sun. The swell of the river lay in the shallow canyon and was a steady growl below them. He led them over and noted how carefully these men took the ford. None of them were easy about it. When they climbed from the shallow canyon, Reno turned toward the low hills of the south. Halfway over the open land, Ganton broke the silence.

"Are you sure this is what you wanna do, Reno? You could get us all killed."

"We'll circle," said Reno. "I've scouted this place. Some of our cattle are in that little valley over there."

They went up a grade and passed into some pines, where Reno turned east with the spine of the ridge and followed it three or four miles, then swung north. He had carefully memorized this country and knew exactly where the cows were.

Now and then through the breaks of the timber he saw cattle grazing below him on Slash A land.

Within another mile he struck an east-west running road. He turned and followed its downgrade, and then they were out in the open.

"Someone's been along here this morning," Ollie Dell remarked.

"Likely," Jim agreed.

Somewhere in the timber's warm and resinous silence, a woodpecker launched its loud attack on a tree, the sound shuddering on and on through the ridge. Far on the northern edge of Slash A grass, Reno made out a cloud of rising dust. They all focused on the small dingy cloud, then scanned the surrounding trees.

"We'll go out there," Jim said, "and round up the vented stuff we find in the nearest bunch. We'll drive it back along this road, straight to the ford. One of you stays here to cover us. Who's the best shot?"

"I am," Patch Meeks said gruffly.

"You stay then, Patch."

Reno led the others out of the trees down the last slope of the hill. He pointed to the herd grazing directly ahead. "Scatter and weed 'em out," he said.

Pack struck off to the left at once. Tuck Wilson went rushing to the other side. Reno himself circled the herd, and they began to cut out the vented animals. Reno heard Wilson and Pack yelling and whistling; Ollie Dell was doing a good, clean job, as he steadily separated out the Sun beef. Within twenty minutes they had their cuts and were moving back toward the ridge.

"Twenty-three," said Ollie. He grinned and brushed the

sweat from his cheeks. His glance kept wandering back to the north, toward the growing ball of dust. He pointed at it and said, "They're comin' up, Jim."

They had the beef at a trot as they reached the ridge's incline, and they were joined by Patch Meeks, who was also watching the dust in the distance. Reno rode forward and found one heifer that had a straight Slash A brand. He cut that cow out and let it drift. Pack Ganton's muddy brown eyes were on him.

"You're particular," he said disdainfully.

"I don't want a rustling charge against us."

"Drivin' this vented stuff home is rustlin' in the valley's judgment."

"Meade's been stealing from us. We're just takin' them back home."

A rare streak of humor crossed Pack Ganton's sullen face. "Maybe," he said, "you ought to hang Meade for being the rustler."

Reno nodded. "That time may come. Somebody's going to hang or die before he gets to the rope."

They moved the cattle steadily along through the timber. Reno said, "Keep behind us a distance, Ollie." He joined the others while Ollie dropped back. The river ford was five miles away, due west, and the sun crawled to the top of the sky. Reno sweated steadily, and his eyes searched the country constantly.

Suddenly Ganton pointed north. "There they come," he announced bitterly.

The dust ball which had been visible far in the distance was much closer now. Reno saw the thin black point of the group coming on and a flash of light against some piece of metal. All of his crew had seen it, and they all rode up beside him, driving the cattle in front. The oncoming group was about a mile away, and Reno stood up in his stirrups and stared. "Looks like there's about six of them," he said.

Pack was nervous and said abruptly, "We better get this straight. What're you gonna do, run or stand? We gonna start shootin' when they get in range?"

"Wait'll they get here," Reno ordered. "It's their choice."

"Well," said Ollie in a matter-of-fact voice, "they're just about here."

The oncoming riders closed the distance, spreading as they approached. Reno heard the steady thud of the horses, and he saw Meade's big body and heard the echo of his voice, though the words were not clear. Reno signaled with his hands, and the crew fanned out, sitting on their horses, waiting.

There were six of them, as Reno had said, and as they rode in, he got a glimpse of Meade's face, anger scoring it. Meade cried out, "Drop your guns!" It was obvious that he expected no trouble, and the men of Slash A fanned out alongside of him, forming a solid line.

Reno sat still, his hands folded on the saddle horn. His legs were straight down in the stirrups, and he was leaning slightly back in the saddle. There was no fear in his stance, and he never took his eyes off the older man. "Meade," he said, "this beef was never sold to you."

"You're a rustler!"

"Show me the bill of sale!" When Meade glared at him, Reno stated flatly, "It never belonged to you, and I'm taking it back. Then I'm gonna comb your range until I get every head that's ours."

"I'll see you hanged!" Meade called in a high, half-strangled voice.

"We're not moving. We're going over that river with this

118

beef. It's up to you to start the fight." Reno was silent for a moment, still staring coldly at Simon Meade, never moving a muscle. He said softly, "Life is pretty sweet, Meade, and a man stays dead for a long time. When you draw—you're dead." Then he added, "But try it if you've got to."

Simon Meade's foreman cried out, "Shoot him down, Mr. Meade!"

Reno said evenly, "Ollie, take Bax if he moves."

A silence fell over the group, and Reno could hear the lowing of the cattle as they moved slowly along. The sky was clear, and the country was wide. But here on this small patch of ground the air of violence held them all still. Reno never ceased watching Simon Meade, whose eyes were clouded with the greatness of his desire to destroy. Reno was guessing that Meade had never been seriously crossed, that his temper had been fed on easy victories. The stand Reno made now was based on that guess, and so he held his motionless attitude and continued to meet that violent stare.

Meade remained silent, and the silence seemed odd to his crew. Finally Bax LeFarge said, "What'll it be, Mr. Meade?"

"Your boss," said Reno easily, "is thinking about staying alive." He continued to study Simon Meade, and he saw the big man's face lose its harsh lines of triumph. He saw doubt creeping in, and he recognized an expression of deep inward shame and a loss of certainty.

Simon Meade took one last look at Reno, then dropped his eyes. He crossed his hands on his saddle horn, studying them, and the corners of his shoulders lost their squareness. His own riders sensed what had happened, and confidence went out of all of them. LeFarge cast a bitter glance at Reno for the destruction he had done and gritted his teeth.

Abruptly Meade turned his horse and rode away, leaving with no command to his men. Bax LeFarge gave Reno one final bitter glance, then muttered, "Let's go," and led the Slash A crew away on Meade's heels.

Reno waited until they were well beyond gunshot. "Now," he said, "let's move on."

They pulled the strayed beef together and moved them westward. As they rode along, Pack Ganton brooded over the clash with Slash A. "I don't understand," he said with some confusion. "I never saw Simon Meade back up before a man."

Reno smiled. "Who's stood up to him lately?"

"Why, I can't rightly remember."

"He was running on a reputation."

"How'd you know that?"

"I made a guess."

Ganton gave him a hard glance, his jaw tightening. "Long chance to take on a guess."

They drove the cattle back, putting them in the fold of a valley close to the ranch house. When they started back for the house, Reno and Ollie rode along together. "I don't understand any more than Pack does," Ollie confessed. "How'd you know Meade would back down?"

Reno liked the boy and wanted him to understand. "It wasn't such a long chance, Ollie," he explained. "A man can be the world's best fighter and still be stopped without a shot. There aren't many men in the world who'll stand in front of another man twenty feet away and risk a pull unless they're dead sure they got a better than even chance. Meade wasn't sure."

Ollie listened carefully, letting it all soak in. Finally he looked at Reno with admiration in his eyes. "Yeah, maybe you're right." Then he added, "But I'll tell you something else. You made a sucker out of Meade. He'll think about that till it turns him crazy. Then he'll go at you in ways that ain't decent. There's a streak in that man. He won't rest now till he's got you fryin' over a fire."

"That may come," said Reno.

★ ★ ★

When Meade led the beaten Slash A crew home, he said not a word and went at once into the house. Bax LeFarge slammed his saddle down in the stable, and Zeno Pounders asked, "What went on out there?"

Bax spit out, "I never saw the old man fold up like that before."

Red DeQueen, another Slash A rider, who had bright red hair and greenish eyes, was as bitter as the rest of the crew. "We had 'em outgunned, Bax! We shoulda just shot 'em down!"

Bax LeFarge wanted to agree; he knew DeQueen was right, but he couldn't go against Simon Meade. All he said was, "We'll take care of those jokers later on." He turned and left the stable and went to the big ranch house. He found Simon Meade standing on the porch, staring off into space. LeFarge said nothing, and finally the hard eyes of Meade focused on him.

Lew Meade came out of the house. "Where have you fellows been?"

LeFarge said bitterly, "We been watching people rustle our beef."

"What!" Lew stared at LeFarge, then at his father. "What's he talking about, Dad?"

Simon Meade's bitterness spilled over. He said venomously, "It's that Reno. He got his crew together and was rustling our stock."

"And you let him do it," Bax muttered under his breath. He couldn't stop the words, though he knew they would arouse Meade's anger—which they did.

"That's enough, Bax!" he roared. "We'll take care of it!"

Lew Meade asked quietly, "It was that vented stock, wasn't it, Dad? I told you we shouldn't have taken those cattle."

Any resistance irritated Simon Meade, and to have it come from his own son was a double grief. Through clenched teeth he said, "I don't understand you, Lew! This is your ranch! It's gonna be one day, anyhow. I've fought Indians and outlaws and rustlers, trying to hold it together so I'd have something to give you. And you act like it's nothing!"

"No, it's not nothing, it's a fine ranch. But what good is it if everybody in the valley hates us? I'd rather have a little goodwill and a few less cows."

Neither Meade nor LeFarge could understand this. To them, it was softness in Lew Meade. Simon Meade shook a meaty fist in the air violently. "If we let the bars down, we'd be eaten alive, boy! Don't you see that? A man's gotta stake his ground and fight for it!"

"I see that! And it looks to me like that's exactly what Reno's doing." His words, he knew, would only fan the fire of anger in his father, but he went on, "You're wrong about all this. I wish you'd learn to be content. We've got the best ranch in the valley, all we need. For the sake of a few more head of beef you're willing to get men killed!" He turned and walked off the porch, saddened by the encounter, knowing that he had little chance of changing his father.

When he was gone, Bax asked insistently, "What're you gonna do about this? They'll come back, you know!"

Simon Meade straightened his broad shoulders. "Put the guns on 'em! Any time you see one of those men, just gun him down! We've gotta show this valley, and especially Jim Reno, that Slash A can't be whipped!"

"It might get rough," LeFarge cautioned. "You sure you're ready to let the party start?"

"You heard me, Bax. From now on, any time you see a man from Sun, it's open season!"

# ELEVEN
*A Time to Dance*

"Mona! Hurry up! We're all ready to go!"

Mona Reynolds peered into the mirror, fixed a small hat over her hair, then considered her image, cocking her head to one side. The light green dress with dark green trim looked becoming. She had only worn it once, and she wondered if it was too dressy for an Independence Day celebration in a western town. She touched the small pearl earrings dangling from her ears, studying her reflection.

Then her mother called out again and she answered, "All right, Mother! I'm coming!" She took time only to put some scent behind her ears and on her throat, then left the room. She found her mother standing in the middle of the parlor, smiling.

"You're not getting ready to go to the White House, Mona! You've been dressing for two hours." Lillian Reynolds' eyes sparkled as she teased her daughter. Then she added, "You look lovely, dear. That dress looks so nice on you."

"Thank you, Mother."

They walked out the door, and found Reno and Chris

standing beside the buggy. "I'm ready," Mona said, and Reno reached out to hand her in while Chris assisted his mother.

"And you look fine, just fine! Both of you!" Chris said proudly.

The two men climbed in, and Reno called out, "Ganton! You and Boone keep an eye on things. It'll be late when we come back."

Ganton merely scowled from where he stood by the fence, one arm hoisted on a fence post. Deacon Boone answered, "You folks have a good time!"

Reno spoke to the horses, and they broke into a fast-paced trot. They were followed by Ollie Dell, Tuck Wilson, and Patch Meeks on horseback. They left the ranch, stirring up a cloud of dust.

The buggy rolled along briskly, the three cowboys angling off to the side to avoid getting their party clothes dusty. Reno said little as they went along, as did Mona, but Chris and Lillian spoke excitedly of the holiday in town. Mona listened with half an ear and was thinking of Reno. She had quarreled with him for four weeks over taking the vented stock from Slash A, but Reno had ignored her and had made several similar visits to surrounding ranches. The result was that Sun Ranch was so well stocked with fresh beef that Reno had remarked that they needed to take on some more riders.

"I don't suppose you're willing to change your mind about taking these vented cattle back, are you, Jim?" Mona asked innocently.

Reno gave her a sidelong glance. "No, Mona. It's a thing that's got to be done. Once a ranch backs up in a place like this, it'll slowly be taken over—or quickly." He shrugged. "There are plenty of ranchers around here who are ready to take our graze. If we're gonna keep it, we've got to stand our ground." He didn't like to talk to her about such things for he knew she felt he was lawless, so he tried to change the subject by saying, "That's a pretty dress you have on. Is it new?"

"No, I've worn it before."

Her brief reply told him that she was not ready for small talk, so he kept his own counsel as the buggy rode along.

When they finally rolled into the main street of Banning, he said, "These folks take their Fourth of July celebration seriously, don't they?" The streets were packed with people, and colored buntings of red, white, and blue festooned the buildings on either side of the broad street. At one end of the town a large platform had been built, and already a band with a banjo, guitar, and fiddle had congregated and was beginning to practice.

Though it was only about two o'clock, the saloons were jam-packed, and the tinny noise of pianos came to Jim as he pulled the buggy up into the lot reserved for wagons and buggies. Jumping down, he helped Mona and Lillian out, saying, "Well, looks like everybody in the country's come to town. Going to be pretty hard to find a meal."

He was right about that, for when they got to the hotel restaurant, it was packed. They had to wait for almost an hour before they could be seated at a table. As they ate, Dave Holly entered, dressed in a light brown suit, accompanied by Belle Montez, who was very striking in a black dress highlighted by spangles, with a mantilla of white lace around her shoulders. Belle nodded at Reno and the Reynoldses, and she and Holly took a table back in one corner.

Lillian glanced at them, then turned to Jim. "Are they supposed to be married?" she inquired.

Jim shrugged, saying, "I don't know, Lillian." His reticence told them this was one of those areas he did not wish them to intrude on.

After the meal, the four of them strolled up and down the street. They observed a shooting contest by the blacksmith's shop, which Chris urged Reno to enter. But Reno merely grinned and shook his head, saying, "I'm out of practice, Chris. You give it a try."

Just then the music started, and Chris said, "No, come on, the dance is starting!" He was looking handsome in a gray suit with a black tie and grinned at his mother. "I'm gonna find me one of these prairie flowers and show her what big city boys can do, Mother!"

Lillian smiled at him fondly. "Better be sure she doesn't have one of these boyfriends that wears hairy chaps and carries two guns, Chris!" Chris laughed as the four of them made their way down to where the dance had started. Already couples were out in front of the platform, and the fiddler was sawing away feverishly.

At once Chris saw a young woman standing over to one side and went to her. The other three couldn't hear what he said, but when he pulled his hat off and spoke to her, her eyes lit up and she nodded. Soon she was dancing with animation, looking up and listening with fascination as Chris spoke.

Mason Deevers appeared and gave a short bow, saying, "I'm going to beat the pack, Mrs. Reynolds. May I have this dance?" Lillian was flustered. She was wearing somber black, but looked very pretty, her delicate features set off by the white shawl she wore. She said, a little nervously, "Oh, I don't think I ought to dance!"

Mona said at once, "Of course you're going to dance!

You're the best dancer I ever saw! Here, let me hold your shawl." She yanked the shawl that was draped modestly about her mother's shoulders and practically shoved her out toward the crowd of dancers, and soon Deevers was guiding her around expertly.

"They make a good-looking couple, don't they," Mona said.

"Sure do," Reno agreed. "Your mother's a fine-looking woman." He almost said, "And you're like her," but he knew that she wouldn't welcome such a statement from him.

At that moment a man planted himself in front of them and spoke. "Howdy," he said heartily. "You're new folks. My name's Jack Bronte." He was six feet tall, sleek and well mus-cled, and had a small mustache that was as black as his hair. He was well dressed; his teeth were very white against his tanned skin. "Not much time to get acquainted in this country, so we just have to introduce ourselves."

"I'm Jim Reno. And this is Miss Ramona Reynolds."

At the name Reno, Bronte's eyes changed, and he studied the smaller man carefully. He put his hand out, though, saying, "Glad to meet you, Reno. Might I borrow your lady friend for a dance?"

Reno shrugged, saying, "Of course, if it's suitable to her."

Mona nodded and gave Bronte a smile. "I'd like that very much." She took his arm, and they went out to join the danc-ers. It was soon obvious that Bronte was an expert dancer. Reno watched them for a while, then turned to the refresh-ment table that had been set up along one of the sidewalks. He got a lemonade and, sipping it slowly, moved back to lean against the wall of one of the buildings. The dance went on, and it seemed as though Bronte was monopolizing Mona.

Lige Benoit, strolling nonchalantly down the sidewalk, stopped and nodded. "Hello, Jim. Came in for the celebration, did you?"

"Sure did."

Benoit's eyes roamed over the dancers, then turned to Reno. There was a tightness about his mouth. "You know him? Bronte?"

"Just met him, Lige."

Benoit was not a talkative man. He had learned too much about the politics of the valley to carry much gossip, but Reno saw that something was troubling him, so he asked, "What's the matter, Lige? Who is this Jack Bronte?"

"A rough one," the sheriff said shortly. Keeping his voice down, he added, "He holes up out in the pocket. That's out west of Sun and Slash A. Wild country out there."

Reno studied the sharp features of Bronte and knew that the sheriff was trying to tell him something. "He a rancher?"

"Well, he handles a lot of cattle," Benoit said, a trace of irony threading his tone, "but that country out there's not made for grazing too many cows. Still, he's shifted quite a few."

Reno sipped his drink casually, but his eyes sharpened because he suddenly understood well what Benoit was saying. If there wasn't grass to graze cows, there was only one way a man could get cattle: either buy them or steal them. He saw that Benoit had turned silent and would say nothing more, so Reno nodded and said briefly, "Thanks, Lige."

The sheriff moved on down the street, shouldering his way through the crowd. Reno watched him idly, his thoughts uncertain as he sipped the warm lemonade. He knew, of course, that Mona had no idea of Jack Bronte's reputation, but on the other hand he didn't feel that he should go cut in on them. He was relieved when, after the dance ended, Mona was claimed by a tall young man with blond hair, and the two went spinning off. He watched Bronte, who moved quietly away and joined several other men, all of whom had rather wild appearances. *A rough one,* the sheriff had said, and as Jim watched the crew he knew that there was something in the words. *They've smelled powder somewhere,* Reno thought steadily. *Have to keep an eye on 'em.*

The dance went on until after dark, when lanterns were lit. The dancers moved by the flickering amber light that gleamed on the jewelry of the women as the music floated along the town's streets. Benoit and his deputies were busy because several partygoers had drunk too much and had to be corralled.

Finally Jim saw Belle standing alone and motionless in the shadows of the bank building. He had watched her as she danced with Holly but had not noticed her dancing with anyone else. A thought came to him, and he made his way to her. She moved slightly as he drew near. Her eyes were black pools in the darkness, but the lights of the yellow lanterns suddenly bloomed in them as she looked up. "Hello, Jim," she said. "I've been watching you. You're not dancing."

"No, I'm not much for that," he said ruefully.

"Will you dance with me?"

Reno blinked in surprise and almost blurted out, "But what about Holly?" But instead he smiled, saying, "Why, sure! Come on."

She took his arm, and they made their way through the crowds to the dancers before the platform. She came into his arms easily, and he found that she moved very gracefully. She said nothing until the dance was well underway, then remarked, "You dance very well, Jim."

"I'm just fair, I guess." He looked at her and saw dissatisfaction in her eyes and face. When the song ended, Reno said, "Let's go get something to drink." They made their way to the refreshment bar, where he finally got some tea. The two of them were so jostled by the crowd that Reno said, "Let's find a place where we're not gonna get stomped. Besides," he complained, "that music's getting on my nerves."

"All right."

She followed him as he led the way through the crowd. They turned a corner and the music suddenly was muted. They walked slowly along the sidewalk, away from the crowds, and came to a tree that for some reason had been allowed to grow off to one side of the street. They stopped, sipping their tea, and Jim began to comment idly on the party. She was silent, though, and finally Jim said, "What's the matter, Belle?"

Looking up at him, she answered quietly, "I think you know."

"He still doesn't want you?"

"I don't know." Anger underscored the bitten-off words. "Sometimes he seems to, and then he comes to me, and he—he looks at me in some way I can't understand. And I know he's thinking about what I've been in the past." There was a plaintive cry in her voice as she said, "Jim, I don't know what to do!"

"Belle, don't let it hurt you so much!" He saw that his words didn't comfort her, and he felt totally inadequate as he stood beside her. Suddenly she dropped her head, her shoulders began to shake, and he saw that she was weeping. Without thinking he put his arms around her and drew her close, saying nothing, just holding her. The gesture seemed to release a fountain, a force within her, and she wept openly, her face pressed against his shoulder. She smelled faintly of lilacs, and there was a fullness to her body that set fire to a deep desire in him. Vaguely he could hear the music, but he could think of nothing but the loveliness of the woman in his arms.

Slowly the tremors ceased. When Belle lifted her face, the tears were like pure silver in her eyes. Her lips were soft and vulnerable. Without thinking, Reno lowered his head and kissed her. There was a hunger in him that had been stirred by her beauty, and she clung to him almost fiercely, holding him tightly. They stood for a long moment. Finally Belle drew back and looked at him, then whispered, "Did that mean anything to you, Jim?"

"A woman's kiss always means something," Reno said, "though I'm no expert." He cupped his hand around her chin. "You've got to make up your mind."

"I've made up my mind," she answered swiftly. "He doesn't want me. I'll have to leave here."

"Running won't help. One place is pretty much like another," Reno said. "But I'm a fool for saying a thing like that—me, who's run all over the country from one place to another trying to find out who I am. Yet here I stand, giving you advice." He took her hand and held it for a moment, then said quietly, "But don't run, Belle. Stay right here and fight it out."

She thought she'd heard something in his voice, an invitation of a sort. Perhaps it was mere hope, perhaps it was the disappointment and disillusionment that had followed her, but whatever it was, she tightened her hand on his, smiled, and said, "I will. I'll stay here for a while, Jim."

He turned, saying, "We'd better get back."

They walked back to the main street and turned toward the dance platform when suddenly Dave Holly appeared. He looked angry and snapped, "Where have you been, Belle? I've been looking for you!" He stared intently at Reno and went on, "You had no call to take Belle away from the party."

"I don't have to answer to you, Dave," Belle retorted.

The shortness of her tone caught Holly up, and his face flushed as anger flooded through him. "It doesn't look good," he protested, "you going off with a man like that, down a side street." He had lost his calmness, and when he looked back at Reno it was obvious he was headed for trouble. "You stay away from her! Haven't you done enough already?"

"You're getting tangled up in your own traces, Holly," Reno said. He had liked the man at first and still felt that basically he was solid, but somehow Holly had gotten himself crossways in his own mind over Belle Montez.

"I don't need any instructions from you, Reno," Holly said shortly and noticed that Belle was staring at him in a peculiar way. There was something in her glance that made him feel less of a man, that he had behaved badly, and the anger that rose in him at his own actions suddenly had to have an outlet. He burst out, "Keep away from her!" and at the same time struck Reno a blow in the chest. He was a strong, powerful man, heavy in the shoulders, and the blow drove Reno backwards.

Belle cried, "Don't be a fool, Dave!" But the sight of Reno staggering backwards and the sound of Belle's cry seemed to loosen something in him, and he leaped after Reno, striking out with all of his might with a powerful right fist.

Reno moved his head so that Holly's fist only grazed his

temple. He grappled with Holly, took a short step to the right, then threw him away. "Cut this out, Holly!" he snapped. "It's not good for Belle."

Holly was in one of those mindless rages that sometimes fall upon a man, and he would not listen to reason. He plunged straight at Jim, throwing punches from every angle. Some of them struck their mark, and Reno was again driven backwards by the furious onslaught. Then Holly missed, and Jim sent a short, powerful blow that caught Holly in the pit of the stomach.

The blow took all the steam out of Holly for a moment, and he clung to Reno, who struggled to free himself. Finally he stepped free and shot a left hand at Dave's face, and it caught the man squarely. Dave fell backwards to the ground but scrambled to his feet almost immediately.

A crowd had begun to gather now, and as always there were catcalls and cries of "Bust him up!" Reno knew he didn't want to wind up in an all-out brawl. He waited until Dave Holly straightened up, then sent one powerful blow that caught Holly right on the point of his chin. It snapped Holly's head back, dropping the man limply to the ground, where he lay without moving.

"Out!" somebody said in astonishment.

Reno's chest was rising and falling, and he stepped over to Belle, saying, "Let's get out of here." He took her away from the crowd, and they walked quickly to the only place he could think of, the hotel. They walked up the stairs without saying a word. When they got to her door she opened it, then turned to look at him, still in silence.

"I'm sorry about all this, Belle," he said. "It won't do you any good."

"It'll do one thing," she answered in a quiet voice. "It'll settle Dave Holly. I won't have to think about that anymore." She sighed, then asked, "Will you come in, Jim?"

"No," he said. "I'll be going now." He didn't turn to leave though, and there was compassion in his fine eyes as he looked at her. "Don't let it get you down. You'll be all right."

"Yes, I'll be all right," she said wearily, then turned and closed the door.

Reno turned and walked down the stairs, angry clear through. *That fool Holly,* he said to himself. *Making a spectacle out of himself and out of Belle! I should've bent a gun barrel over his head!*

★  ★  ★

When Dave Holly came to, he found the sheriff looking at him. He was sitting in a chair on the sidewalk, and Benoit said quietly, "Do I have to throw you in jail to keep you from going after Reno again, Holly?"

"No." The recent events left a bitter taste in his mouth, and he knew he'd made a fool of himself. "All I want to do is get out of here, Lige."

He got to his feet, found his hat and put it on, then walked unsteadily away. He walked to his mount, slowly got into the saddle, then put the spurs to the buckskin and rode away. The hot summer breeze in his face did nothing to cool him off. He knew he'd made one of the worst mistakes he'd made in his whole life.

The fight seemed to have settled several things. Chris found Reno and said, "It's time to go, I guess." He gave Jim a sidelong glance and went on, "Mona's pretty mad, Jim. She thinks you should've stayed out of that."

"She's probably right," Reno said.

They got into the buggy and went back to the ranch, leaving the crew in town for the rest of the celebration. Very little was said on the way back, but when they got home, Mona said as Jim helped her down, "I want to have a word with you."

"All right." Reno waited until Chris and Lillian went into the house, then turned to face her. "OK, let's hear the sermon."

"You're making a joke out of this ranch, chasing around after that woman! It's got to stop! Do you hear me, Jim Reno?"

Reno was angry now, and said without thinking, "Good thing that you've never made a mistake, Mona! That you've never done anything wrong in your whole life! That you've always behaved just exactly like you ought to! Too bad us mortals can't be that well behaved!"

He wheeled suddenly and walked away, leaving her standing alone. Then, without another word, she turned and stalked into the house, angry to the bone.

# TWELVE
## *The Trouble Begins*

Late afternoon had broken the heat of the day when Lew Meade turned his horse homeward. He passed over the hilly land of rolling grass, separated by ridges into independent valleys, and caught the scent of pines in the air. He continued until he came to the river, waded his horse across it, then looked up sharply as he saw another rider coming from out of the timber to the west. Looking closely he saw that it was Mona Reynolds. Spurring his horse forward to meet her, he pulled up with a flourish, tugged the brim of his hat, and said cheerfully, "Good afternoon!"

Mona was wearing a divided riding skirt of dark brown, a white silk blouse that fit her neatly, and a small-brimmed black hat held on by a leather lanyard. "Hello, Lew," she said. Looking over to the north she asked, "You're a little bit off of your range, aren't you?" There was a coolness in her voice as she studied him. He had danced with her several times at the celebration two weeks earlier and had been friendly and cheerful, and she had rather liked him. But now in the clear light of the afternoon she was reminded that he was the son of Simon Meade, their enemy.

Meade read her at once and said gravely, "Guess I know what you're thinking, Mona. But you're wrong—about me at least. Can I ride with you a little way along the river?"

"I suppose so."

As the two rode along, Meade made his case as well as he could. "I've told you before, Mona, my dad and I don't see alike on this thing. I've told him the ranch we've got is big enough and that we've got more cattle than we can handle." He pushed his hat back, eyes searching the horizon, and murmured, "I wish Dad was more like he was when my mother was alive."

A look of sorrow crossed Mona's face. "How did she die, Lew?"

The question seemed to trouble Lew Meade. "Well, she died when I was real young. She was on a trip to see her people—and a war party of Sioux made a raid. They killed her and made off with my brother." He stared down at his hands, his lean face suddenly very sober. When he looked up there was grief in his eyes. "I was just a kid, Mona, but I can remember how gentle she was. My dad almost went crazy—struck out to kill any Indians he could find when he heard about her and my little brother. He spent years looking for Jason, but he never found him."

"How awful!"

Meade looked at her, then shook his head. "Dad was never the same. He got mean and hard. Before Mother died, he was always laughing. I can remember he took me to town with him, bought me candy. But afterwards, he never laughed." He hesitated, then added, "That's no excuse for his ways, Mona, but I've regretted a long time that she died. Dad would have been different, I think."

"I'm sorry."

He shrugged, adding, "He's tried to build a big ranch for me. But what good is a big ranch? Man can only wear one suit and can only ride one horse at a time." He gave her a sidelong glance and grinned. "And he can only have one woman. So why would anybody want two of anything?"

"You fool." Mona was amused and laughed lightly. But he had the power to charm her, and she realized that there was a vast distance between Lew Mcadc and his father.

They wandered along the river, and he spoke of more pleasant things. As they approached Sun Ranch he said wryly, "I guess I better cut around. Reno might give me a pretty hot reception. He's been dealing all the ranchers a pretty hard time, going after the vented cattle."

"They're our cattle," Mona said shortly. Reno had at last instilled this into her. Her lips tightened resolutely, which did not make her any less attractive, Lew thought. She was a firm girl and decisive in her ways, but he liked that in a woman. She went on, "Let's not quarrel about it, Lew. We can never be close; there's too much between us."

"Wouldn't be too sure about that." He tipped his hat, smiled at her, and said, "I'll be seeing you again, Mona." Then he spurred his horse and galloped off.

He kept his horse at a fast gait and covered the territory along the river, thinking of Mona and how he felt about her. He had known women before, but something about this one drew him. It was not just because she was beautiful, although that certainly was a factor. But there was something in her that he had not found in the other young women of the community.

He pulled into Slash A just at dusk, went straight to the barn, unsaddled his horse, grained him, and walked slowly back to the house, thinking mostly about Mona. He stopped short when he saw his father standing on the front porch, Jack Bronte beside him. A slight coolness touched his features, and he said shortly, "Hello, Jack," and passed into the house, murmuring a greeting to his father.

As the door slammed, Jack Bronte, who was lounging against a post, stared after him and grinned rakishly at Simon Meade. "I don't reckon Lew cares much for me, Simon," he said.

Simon Meade said impatiently, "Never mind that. Now, I want to get this thing clear."

"It's clear enough." Bronte eyed the huge man with the white hair speculatively and thought, *He's a tough old bird, but he's feeling his age.* Then he went on, "You've sent for me because you don't have anybody else to send for. I never thought I'd see the day, I admit, when you'd call for help from anybody."

Meade, still sensitive about his defeat at the hands of Jim Reno, said gruffly, "It's a business deal, Bronte. Nothing more. Now, you got it straight?"

"Sure. You want me to rustle Sun cattle so that those folks go broke over there. That it?"

"Call it anything you want to," Meade said harshly. "I want 'em off that place, and they can't stay if they don't have a herd."

Bronte pulled slowly at the lobe of one ear thoughtfully, yet there was a deadly air about him. He was an outlaw but had never been caught. Everyone in the valley knew what he was, but he just laughed at them and outlasted every attempt to bring him to justice. The country where he worked—back in the pocket—was so wild that no one cared to follow his tracks back there, and anyone going too far into his territory was likely to hear a warning shot. It was quite like a medieval stronghold, where he ruled as an absolute monarch. Now he shrugged carelessly and said, "I'll have to get more out of it than a few cows."

"What do you want?" Meade demanded.

"All of Sun east of Deer Creek."

"Why don't you just ask for all of it?" Meade asked sarcastically.

Bronte shrugged. "Because I'm not big enough to take all of it."

"I can get someone else to take care of this chore!"

"Better get someone pretty fast with a gun. Reno's not easy. Better get somebody who can pull faster than he can. And I guess I'm the only one that's sure about that." He was growing restless and stepped off the porch.

Meade said grudgingly, "All right, it's a deal."

"Right. I'll start moving the stuff off right away. If they give us any trouble, we may have to lay a few of them in the dust."

"Just do what I've told you to do," Meade said with finality. Turning abruptly, he went into the house. He was tense, for he had never called upon any man for help, much less an outlaw such as Jack Bronte.

He went into the kitchen, where he found Lew putting together a sandwich of cold beef and mustard. When Lew did not speak, Meade demanded, "Well, spit it out! I know what you're thinking!"

Lew stared at him. Lew had never been much of a serious man; rather, he was lighthearted and had always gone his own way, doing only enough work to keep himself clear of the charge of being a loafer. But now he was twenty-four and thinking more seriously. "All right," he said, "I will. I don't know what Jack Bronte's doing here, but don't have anything to do with him, Dad."

"He can be useful," Meade said. And because he felt strange about allying himself with Bronte he spoke brusquely, almost angrily. "You're afraid to get your hands dirty, Lew, that's your trouble!" There was a bitter light in Meade's eyes, and his mouth turned down in a scowl. "You've had everything handed to you on a silver platter. Now things are coming up tough, and I don't think you've got it in you to hold this ranch together."

Lew Meade laid the sandwich down, finding it distasteful. He got to his feet and faced his father. "Any time Slash A has to use people like Jack Bronte," he said curtly, holding his father's eyes, "it's not much of a ranch." Then he turned and walked out of the room, leaving his father speechless.

Simon Meade suddenly struck the wall a mighty blow that sent a picture on one of the shelves crashing down to the floor, the glass frame shattering into smithereens. He stared blankly at the door, angry and afraid. He had one thing to live for, and that was Slash A. Since his wife had died he had been a lonely man, but he had looked to the day when he and his son would rule this cattle empire together. Now he knew that was slipping away from him.

★ ★ ★

The first indication any of them had that anything was wrong came just after breakfast the next morning. As usual, Reno was eating with the family, explaining his plan to sell off part of the herd so they wouldn't have to winter so many. "If we can get rid of the worst that we've got," he was saying, "we can keep the best on what grass there is. Then, come next spring—"

"Look!" Chris interrupted. "There comes Ollie, riding like the devil's after him!" He jumped up and ran to the door, opening it just in time for Ollie to fall through it. "What's the matter, Ollie?" Chris asked anxiously.

"The devil to pay, that's what's the matter!" Ollie Dell was dusty from head to foot and had obviously ridden hard.

Jim got up and walked around the table, asking, "What is it, Dell?"

"You know them thirty head we had over by the river where that creek comes into it? Where the big oak tree swings out over it?"

"Yeah, I know the place, Ollie," Jim said patiently. "What's wrong?"

Ollie wiped his mouth and took a deep breath. "Well, the cattle are gone, that's what's the matter!" he said in a tight voice. His sharp blue eyes flashed with anger, and he snapped, "And they didn't walk away by themselves, either! I followed their tracks quite a way, and there's shod horsemen takin' 'em somewheres!"

"Which direction were they headed?"

Ollie looked at Reno, then said, "It looks like they were headed straight towards the pocket."

Reno was already almost out the door. "Go saddle a fresh horse, Ollie. We'll go have a look."

"Can I come too, Jim?" Chris asked.

Reno looked at him, glanced at Lillian, then said, "It might be better if you didn't. I don't know what we'll run into out there. That's rough country."

Chris's lips drew into a firm line, and his eyes grew defiant. "How am I ever going to learn if you don't ever give me a chance? I'm not a baby! C'mon, let me go, Jim!"

Jim knew what was going on in the boy's heart and mind. He remembered when he himself had been seventeen and in the Confederate army. He didn't want to be left out of anything, and he had to prove himself a man, which didn't take long at that time. He looked again at Lillian and asked simply, "Lillian?"

Lillian Reynolds wanted to say no with finality, but she had grown knowledgeable about the West in the few months they had been in Wyoming. She had already seen her son give up some of his spoiled, childish ways, and although she knew that danger was out there, she also had talked enough with Jim and with Deacon Boone to learn that young men had to endure hardship and even danger in order to grow up in this country. "All right, Chris," she said, "go ahead." Chris gave her a grateful look, ran over and kissed her, then dashed out of the room to get his riding clothes on.

Reno hurried out of the house, saddled a tall, rangy bay, and then saddled Chris's horse. By the time he was finished Chris was there, a .44 strapped onto his hip. "Better put a rifle in that boot," Reno said, as he shoved his own Winchester into position. Down at the end of the barn Ollie had saddled up, and Jim said, "You ready to go, Ollie?"

"Sure."

The three of them rode out and struck due south. As they went, Mona stood on the porch and watched them. Everything in her rebelled at this sort of thing, and she turned to face her mother. "I don't think you should've let Chris go. He could get hurt."

"I can't keep him a baby forever, Mona. He's seventeen years old, and that's a man out here." As she watched the three riders disappear she went on, "You know, I was just thinking. Your father would have been very proud of Chris. He was always afraid he was going to turn out to be less than a man." Her eyes grew misty, and her lower lip trembled a little despite herself as she said softly, "We all are going to have to change, Mona." Turning to face her daughter she said, "You've given Jim a hard time, and I haven't said much, but I'm telling you it's got to stop."

Mona exclaimed, "Why, Mother—"

"He's risking his life for us here. He doesn't have any investment in this place; he's just doing it for the family of a man that he loved and respected. And all he gets from you," she said sternly, "is hard, harsh words. I'm disappointed in you." Then she turned and walked into the house.

Mona blinked in surprise. Her mother had never spoken to her like that, and perhaps she had felt some of the same thing herself, for a wave of guilt rushed over her. She knew she had been harsh with Reno, and now that her mother had put it into words she felt keenly the wrong she might have been doing the man. She looked again as the cloud of dust raised by the three riders was fading into the west and thought, *I'll have to do better. When he gets back, I'll be different.*

★ ★ ★

Lige Benoit was sitting in his cane-backed chair, tilted back against the outer wall of his office, watching the late afternoon sun slowly sink beyond the hills. It was his favorite time of day. The town wasn't stirring yet as it would be a little later on when the saloons got crowded. The merchants had mostly closed up and gone to their homes. A peacefulness rested on Banning.

He lifted his eyes and was surprised to see three horse-men come in. He made them out to be Jim Reno accompanied by the Reynolds boy and one of the Sun riders, Ollie Dell. Slowly he let his chair down and studied the men. He'd been a lawman long enough and had lived in the West long enough to read the signs as they appeared. His black eyes were hooded as he watched the men lead their tired horses slowly down the street. He realized that they were coming in his direction and thought, *Nobody ever comes to see Ol' Lige unless there's trouble. Now what can those boys be up to?*

He got to his feet as the three led their horses up to the rail and looped the reins around it. "What's wrong?" he asked. "You boys look all beat out."

Reno took his hat off and drew his arm across his brow, wiping the sweat away. His face was flushed with the heat, as were the faces of the other two. Then he said, "Came in to talk to you, Lige. Maybe ask a favor."

"Step in. You boys look dried out. I got some water inside." The three men followed Benoit into the office. He found three cups and poured some water out of the olla and watched as they drank thirstily. He filled their cups several times.

Reno finally lowered his cup and said, "Thanks, Lige. I was so dry I was spittin' cotton." He put the cup down deliber-ately and went on, "I know it's out of your jurisdiction, but we've had some rustling out at Sun."

"Know who did it?" Benoit asked sharply. He was very alert to any trouble in the valley, knowing that sooner or later it would come to town, and he would have to handle it. He knew they were all sitting on a powder keg, with the free grass being claimed, pitting rancher against rancher. He expected and dreaded to hear Reno's report that one of the ranchers had taken the Sun cattle.

Reno's eyes locked with Benoit's cold gaze, and he said in a low voice, "They were driven up into the pocket."

"Oh. The pocket."

Reno saw that the sheriff well understood what he had been told. "That's right. We followed them up as far as Willow Creek, but when we got to that canyon, somebody started shooting at us from up top."

"None of you got hit?" Benoit asked, looking all of them up and down quickly.

"No," Ollie put in, "but we would've been if we'd gone any further." His youthful face was red with sunburn, but his lips looked almost pale; it had been that dry and hot a day. "I wanted to go up after 'em but Jim wouldn't go for it. He said they'd cut us down."

"Jim's right. That's bad country," Benoit said. He turned and studied Jim, taking in the toughness of Reno's face, and knew that whoever had taken the Sun cattle hadn't heard the last of it. "You did the right thing, pulling back," he told Jim. "That's a terrible place for an ambush in those canyons out there. All three of you could've gotten killed."

Reno observed, "In that you're right." His words were said with almost an air of relaxation, but there was a tenseness in his muscles that gave away his intention. "I wanted to tell you, Lige, that we'll be going after those cattle. Since it is out of your jurisdiction, if you want to call in a federal marshal, that's fine with me."

"Doubt they'd come," Benoit said succinctly. "They got a lot of territory to cover, and there's just not enough to warrant bringing one in right now."

"Maybe a few dead men would bring one in," Ollie snapped. He turned and said, "I'm goin' down to the saloon and get something to drink, Jim. C'mon with me."

Benoit hooked his thumbs in his gun belt and said, "You two young fellas go on. I need to talk to Jim."

Jim nodded, and the two left. He turned back to Benoit and asked, "What is it, Lige? Don't try to tell me not to go into the pocket. I know Bronte took those cattle. I can't prove it, but I know it. Who else would be going up there?"

"You're probably right," Benoit agreed. "But it wasn't that I wanted to talk to you about. You haven't been into town in a week, Jim. You didn't hear about Belle Montez?"

Instantly Reno looked alert and said, "No. What happened?"

"She got sick three days ago. Some kind of fever. Doc Hardy doesn't know what it is. She's been lying up there in her room all this time. The waitress has been taking food up to her, but the doc's been gone a lot. He said she wasn't doin' good at all and needed to be where she could get better care."

"What about Holly? Does he know about it?"

"He rode out of here after that fight you and him had, and nobody's seen him since. I reckon he's out at his ranch poutin' or something. He sure made a fool out of himself!" Benoit snorted disgustedly. "Anyway, I thought you might want to know about it, Jim." His eyes were idly roaming the office. "I think a lot of that girl. Some of the townspeople look down on her, her bein' kind of a mail-order bride—and then that fight you and Holly had. But I tell you, she's a fine woman."

"Yes, she is, Lige." Jim stood, uncertainty on his face, mentally trying one answer and then another, then disregarding them all. Finally he asked, "And none of the people here in town offered to take her in?"

Benoit looked slightly embarrassed. "Well, not really. One of the saloon keepers said she could have a room, but it was the Blue Moon, and you know what kind of a place that is. She wouldn't want to go there."

"No," Reno said hastily. He thought for a minute, then said, "I'll take her out to Sun. Lillian Reynolds is a good woman, and I expect she can be a good nurse, too."

Relief washed over Benoit's face. "I was hoping you'd say that. Mrs. Reynolds sure does seem like a fine woman, and there's that girl, Ramona, too. They ought to be able to take care of her." He went on with uncharacteristic eagerness, "You can use my wagon if you want to, and I'll have a bed put in the back so she'll have an easy trip."

"All right, Lige. I'll go get her if you'll get the wagon." He studied Benoit for a moment, then smiled. "You're kind of tough to be a Santa Claus. Never knew a town sheriff to have such tender mercies."

"Ah, get outta here, Jim. You're just as bad." Benoit walked past him and turned down the street.

Reno went the other way toward the saloon to tell Chris and Ollie what had happened. "I'm taking Belle back for your mother and sister to take care of," he said. "You two can come with us if you want to."

"Naw, we're staying for a little while," Ollie said. "We need to get a little more of this liquid refreshment down us. I'm turned to dust. Ain't that right, Chris?"

Chris ignored Ollie and was looking at Reno doubtfully. "I don't know how Mona will take it, Jim. She's kinda funny."

Reno merely shrugged and said, "She'll be all right, I hope. But anyway, your mother'll do the right thing."

He turned and left the saloon and went at once to the

hotel, ascended directly to the second floor, and knocked on Belle's door.

"Come in," he heard a voice say weakly.

Opening the door, he found Belle lying in bed, covered with a blanket. She looked pale, and as he walked toward her he saw that her cheeks and eyes were sunken in.

"What's all this?" Jim said gently, laying his hand awkwardly on her forehead and leaving it there for a moment. "You don't have any fever right now."

Belle stared up at him and said tiredly, "It comes and goes. What are you doing here, Jim?"

He said firmly, "I came to take you out to Sun. You can't stay here in this place all alone, Belle."

"I can't go there; I won't." Belle's dull eyes grew alarmed, and her weak voice took on a frantic note. She began to protest, "I'll be all right! Just leave me alone!"

"Look, Belle," he said, "there are two ways you can go. Either kickin' and screamin', or you can let me carry you down and put you in the wagon like a lady. But it's gonna be one or the other. Now, which will it be?"

Belle stared at him and smiled in spite of herself. She had been so sick and now was so weak she wasn't even sure she could sit up, much less kick and scream. "I guess I'll be a lady," she said faintly.

"All right. Now, where're your suitcases?" Quickly Reno gathered all of her things, filled her luggage, and then said, "I'll carry your things down. Can you slip into this robe while I'm gone?"

Belle waited until he left with her trunk and suitcases, then threw the cover back. She sat up slowly and swayed, closing her eyes against the dizziness that came to her. She slipped into the robe and had managed to stand up by the time Jim came back.

"That's a good girl," he said. "Now, you just let ol' Doc Reno take care of you." He reached down, picked her up, and said, "Hang on to me now. Benoit's got a nice bed made for you in the back of his wagon." He started down the stairs, and Belle held on to him, pressing her face against his chest. She felt very small, almost like a little girl again. She closed her eyes as they passed through the lobby, not wanting to see anyone.

Outside the darkness was falling. Jim said, "Here she is, Lige. Help me get her into the wagon."

Benoit leaped up into the wagon, took Belle from Jim, lifting her easily, and carefully laid her down. As he covered her with some blankets, he said, "You'll be fine out at Sun, Miss Belle. I'll be checkin' on you." He jumped back to the ground, and Reno clapped him on the shoulder, then got into the wagon seat and drove away.

As the sound of the wagon faded into the night Benoit thought, *That's sure a good fella.* He looked after the wagon, then reflected, *But he's sure headed for a heap of trouble.*

★ ★ ★

Lillian heard the sound of the wagon stopping out front, so she put her sewing down and walked to the door. It was very late, and she was worried about the men. She opened the door and saw Reno getting down out of a wagon—not theirs—with his horse hitched to the back. "What is it, Jim? We've all been worried about you! Where are the others?"

"Chris and Ollie will be along pretty soon. They're in town." He stopped in front of her and pulled his hat off. "Lillian, Belle Montez has been real sick. Got some kind of a fever, and there's nobody to take care of her." He hesitated, then went on, "I brought her here. I thought you might be willing to help."

Lillian was surprised, but what she said proved how much she had changed. "Why, of course! Bring her into the house, Jim. We'll put her in the room at the end of the hall. I'll get it ready."

She started to turn toward the bedroom, but Reno's voice stopped her. "This really is very kind of you. I do appreciate it."

Lillian smiled at Reno, then headed for the bedroom. She was turning the bed down when Jim carried the woman in. "Put her right here, Jim," she said. "Now, you get out of here. I'm going to give her a nice cool bath. I can see she needs it." Looking down at Belle, she said soothingly, "How are you? I'm glad Jim brought you, Belle. You need someone to take care of you. I know what it is to be sick."

Belle, blinking back the tears that leaped into her eyes, whispered, "Thank you," and then looked at Jim. "And thank you, Jim."

"You'll be all right." Belle's intense gaze disturbed Reno, and he said quickly, "You know, I've always wanted to get sick myself so Lillian could take care of me." Then he turned and left the room.

# THIRTEEN
### "You're No Son of Mine!"

As Dave Holly rode into Banning shortly before noon, he heard a voice call his name. "Hey, Holly!"

He turned and saw Sheriff Benoit standing with two men in front of his office and pulled his horse up abruptly. "Come on over here!" Benoit commanded.

With a sigh Holly turned his horse across the street to stop in front of the three men. Remaining in the saddle, he looked down at the sheriff and asked belligerently, "What is it, Lige?" In his mind he was reliving the moment when he awoke after being beaten by Reno and the first man he'd seen had been Benoit. He knew that the sheriff and others in the town thought less of him—not only for the fight, but for having engaged in a romance with a woman he didn't even know. "I'm in a hurry," he said brusquely.

"I guess you ain't heard about Belle, have you, Dave?"

Holly stared at him and asked in a less belligerent manner, "Heard what?"

"She got sick a few days ago, and there wasn't any place

to put her here in town, so she's out at Sun Ranch now. Mrs. Reynolds and that girl are taking care of her."

A sense of frustration swept over Holly, and he thought angrily, *It's Reno again! He's after her!* He tried to let none of this show on his face, but he was aware that he was a poor hand at keeping his emotions hidden. He forced himself to say, "Thanks, Sheriff. I hadn't heard about that. I'll go out and see how she is right now."

As Holly started to turn away, Benoit said, "These two fellas are headed out to Sun. This here is Easy Jones, and this young buck is Lee Morgan. They're friends of Reno's from Montana. Thought you wouldn't mind lettin' 'em ride along with you, show 'em the way."

Holly glanced at the two, noting that the one was short, slight, and bandy-legged but still had a tough look about him. The other was a boy with bright blue eyes, tall but gangly and awkward. He wondered about the two, but shrugged and said, "Sure. Come on along."

Easy said, "Thanks, Sheriff," and the two mounted their horses, which were tied at the rail. As Holly moved down the street toward the edge of town Easy said, "Nice of you to show us the way, Holly. Me an' Lee are pretty bad to get lost, ain't we boy?" He grinned at the boy, who frowned and denied everything.

As they rode south, Easy talked freely, but Holly replied only briefly. As the two spoke, Holly picked up the fact that they had been in the gold mining country. He listened carefully for any trace of talk about Reno, and as far as he could tell the three were not related. Late that afternoon he pulled his horse up and nodded, "That's Sun Ranch down there."

Easy and Lee looked down at the spread, and the boy said, "That's a fine ranch, ain't it, Easy?"

"Sure is, boy! C'mon, let's go find that Mr. James Reno and give him a piece of our mind!"

The three moved along, and Mona Reynolds stepped outside onto the front porch as they approached. She nodded to Holly, saying, "Hello, Mr. Holly." She then set her eyes on the other two.

"These two fellows are looking for Reno," Holly said. "Friends of his from Montana."

"He's out with the crew," Mona said. "If you follow the river over there, I think you'll find them about five miles downstream."

"Thanks, miss, we'll just go lookin'," Easy said, and when they were out of Mona's earshot, he grinned at Lee. "Well, I mighta knowed Jim Reno'd have a pretty gal on the place somewhere. Prettier than a speckled pup, ain't she, boy?"

They followed the river that wound around the valley and soon saw some cattle milling around with two riders moving them along. Easy squinted his eyes and said, "That's him. That's Mr. James Reno right there, boy."

Lee stared, then shook his head, as always amazed by the keenness of his companion's eyesight. "I don't know how you can see so far, Easy," he complained. There was a worried look on his face, and he said, "I don't think Jim's gonna be too happy about seein' us."

"Aw, who wouldn't be glad to see us?" Easy grinned. He spurred his horse, and the two rode forward at a gallop. As they approached Reno, Easy raised his hat and called, "Hey there, you jaybird! It's us!"

Reno had seen them coming and turned his horse toward them. As they met, he grinned and said, "I thought I put you two to work grubbing in the dirt to make me rich and famous!"

"Aw, you're rich and famous enough, Jim! Problem is, you just ain't as good-lookin' as I am!" Easy answered. He patted his horse and went on, "We done worked ourselfs down on that durn ol' gold mine! And when we got your letter, it sounded like you might be needin' some help. We let Pat Fairleigh mind the claim on fifty-fifty, and here we are!"

"I hope you ain't mad about us leavin, Jim," Lee spoke up anxiously, "but it sure did get lonesome out there without you."

Reno smiled at the boy. "No, I'm real glad to see both of you. I don't have enough to do around here," he added, "so I need two more worthless riders to take care of. Come on, we've gotta get these steers moved, and then we'll get back to the ranch." As the three men rode toward the slow-moving herd, Reno guided his horse up close to Lee and reached out and slapped him on the shoulder, saying affectionately, "I missed you."

After a moment of silence, Reno asked, "I don't suppose I have a right to ask, but how's Rachel doing?"

"Well, James," Easy answered, "she was draggin' 'round like a lonesome pup for a while, but she was doin' better when we left. We told her hello like you asked us in your letter."

"And?"

"She said to say hello."

"Was that all, Easy?" Reno asked, not sure if he really wanted her to say more.

"Yep, James, that was all."

"Oh." Disappointment crossed Reno's face, but he knew he had no one to blame but himself. He looked at the herd, then yelled out, "What're we waitin' for? Let's get these beef movin'!" Reno spurred his horse and began herding the cattle.

★ ★ ★

After the two men had ridden off, Dave Holly suddenly felt very awkward. Mona gazed curiously at him, and he said uncomfortably, "I didn't hear about Belle being sick until this morning, so I came right over. How is she?"

"Still pretty weak and not over that fever yet," Mona answered. "Come on in, and I'll see if she's awake." Holly followed her into the house and waited while she disappeared down the short hall, then returned. "It's all right. You can go on in."

"Thanks, Miss Reynolds."

Dave entered the room and found Belle sitting up in bed. She had on a rose-colored gown and some sort of short jacket over it. Her hair was down, flowing over her shoulders and the white pillow that propped her up. "Hello, Belle," he said sheepishly. There was a chair beside the bed, and he walked over to sit down, putting his hat clumsily on the floor. "I came as soon as I heard you were sick," he said. "You should've sent word to me."

Belle's face was pale from the sickness, and there were hollows in her cheeks, showing that she had lost weight. Nevertheless he thought she looked even more beautiful. As she observed him, she could not identify her own feelings and said only, "I'm sorry I didn't send you word, Dave, but I didn't have anyone to send."

Holly listened to her words, trying to find something in them that showed that she blamed him. Then he took a deep breath and blurted out, "I made a fool of myself at that dance, Belle. I didn't have any business blowing up like that. I'm sorry."

Belle had been upset and angry with Holly over his behavior, but his straightforward, honest apology made her feel better. She smiled, saying kindly, "That's all right, Dave. We all do things like that at times."

Her words relieved Holly, and he went on, "I wish I didn't have this temper. I walk around with it all the time, but sometimes it just gets away from me." He clasped his hands and leaned forward, concern in his hazel eyes. "Are you all right? I mean, you're getting better, ain't you?"

"Oh, yes. Mrs. Reynolds has taken such good care of me." She smiled, adding, "I think she's a natural-born nurse. And Mona's been a help, too."

She listened as Dave told her what he'd been doing at his ranch. It seemed to her that he was taking great care to give her details, and she saw an eagerness in him that she had not seen before.

After a while he grew silent and seemed to be struggling to say something. His mouth twisted, and the words came out slowly. "Belle, I've behaved pretty bad. Didn't think I could be so dumb. But I just want you to know, I stand ready to keep our bargain."

That didn't sound right, even to him. It made their marriage sound something like a financial agreement or a partnership in a business. He was not a man who was good with words, and even though he had been feeling more and more strongly about this woman, he could not find the words he knew she wanted to hear. He tried again, saying, "I mean, it'll take awhile to get the ranch ready for a woman to come, but—"

"Dave," Belle said quietly, "I've had a lot of time to think since I've been sick, and it's come to me that we were too hasty. A marriage has to be more than just a man and a woman living together. There has to be a firmer foundation than that."

Holly thought of the man she had been going to marry and how he had told her that he could never give her what that man had given her. Frustrated and tongue-tied, he tried to think, but his thoughts were wild and disjointed. He could only nod and say, "I'm not giving up, Belle, but I'll wait till you're better before we talk about it again."

They talked some more, and it was Belle who finally brought up the precarious standing of Sun Ranch. She said, "Jim tells me that they're being rustled heavily. Men riding out of the hills in small bunches, and there's not enough of a crew to watch all the herds. He says there's going to be a fight."

"I wish he wouldn't talk like that, although I guess that's how it is," Holly said regretfully. "There'll be a fight. Meade's not going to give up—and there are others who'd like to have a part of this ranch, too."

"Are you one of them, Dave?"

"No! I've got all the ranch I want. And besides, I agree with Reno about one thing, about this being an owned ranch. It was different when Reynolds wasn't here. No cattleman likes to see range go empty, but now, as far as I'm concerned, Sun Ranch belongs to the Reynoldses."

Belle reached her hand out and placed it on the broad hand of Dave Holly. "I'm glad you said that, Dave," she said softly. "Sun's going to need all the friends it can get. And they've been so nice to me here. I'd hate it if Lillian and her family had to leave this place; they don't have anywhere else to go." She hesitated, then said, "Like me, I guess. Maybe that's why I feel like I do about them."

Holly wanted to say, "You do have a place to go," but simply couldn't get the words out. Instead he muttered, "Meade's never going to be satisfied, but I'll contact some of the ranchers, and maybe we can talk some sense into him."

The time ran on and Belle, who knew how to draw a man out, lay there smiling and listening and soon had Dave talking about how he came out west and built up his ranch from almost nothing. As he talked she thought, *This is a good man, and I could have him. But do I want him?* And she discovered that she had no answer to that question.

★　★　★

The argument that flared up between Lew Meade and his father was totally unexpected to both of them. Lew had been branding cattle out on the south meadows. He returned wearily to the ranch house, put his horse up in the barn, and went into the house to get a cup of milk to wash down the dust of the trail.

He heard horses coming, and when he looked out the window he saw Bax LeFarge and his father ride in and dismount. They were talking intently and did not suspect anyone was within earshot.

LeFarge said, "You gotta do it, Simon. It's not enough to have Bronte nibblin' away at their herds. Sooner or later he's gonna get caught. And even if he does get the cattle, how's that gonna help us?"

"It'll help us if he thins them down to where they have to sell out," Simon Meade said. "What do you think we ought to do, Bax?"

"I think we oughta hit 'em with everything we've got," LeFarge said savagely. He was a rough man in every way— appearance, mannerisms, voice. A brutal man, he was known to have killed two men in his earlier days.

As Lew stood motionless, listening, he realized again how much he disliked Bax LeFarge. He had tried several times to persuade his father to get rid of him, but Simon had always simply said, "He's tough, but that's what we need here at Slash A to keep this bunch in line." Lew had put the milk down on the table and stood listening quietly as the two continued to speak.

LeFarge said, "They ain't got but a handful over there. What we need to do is ride out of here tonight, hit 'em hard, and take those cattle out west. We can let Bronte handle 'em when we get 'em to the pocket. Any blame for the rustlin' will fall on him."

"I don't know if Bronte will go for that."

"He'll go for anything that's got a dollar in it," LeFarge snapped. "You know that, Simon." His voice grew even uglier as he went on. "I'm tired of Reno lording it over us. He put the run on us once, and nobody in the valley's ever gonna forget that. I hope you ain't!"

"No, I haven't." There was a sad note, Lew thought, in his father's voice. "First time a man ever made me take water." Then after a moment he spoke again, with anger. "I'll think about it, Bax. But not now."

LeFarge snorted and walked off, and Simon Meade entered the house. He had no sooner gotten inside when Lew walked out of the kitchen to confront him. "Dad," he said, "you can't do it."

Meade looked up, glanced toward the kitchen, and realized that his son had overheard his conversation with Bax LeFarge. His anger flared up, and he said, "Lew, we won't talk about this. As long as I'm alive, I'm running this ranch. You just do your work."

Lew Meade stood there, and a great wave of disappointment washed over him. He had known for years that his father was an overbearing man, but this was different. It had been hard keeping a big ranch together, and up until now he had been rather proud of the toughness of Slash A. But something about the change that had come over his father since Reno had come to town, since Sun Ranch had become an issue, saddened him. He knew now that he was being dismissed, and he felt it was one of those times in a man's life when he has to make a decision. He realized he would never change his father's mind with talk, and yet at the same time he could not face the idea of joining up with outlaws like Jack Bronte.

Lew Meade took a deep breath and said slowly, "I guess you've forgotten one thing. I'm twenty-four years old, and if I'm not fit to have a say in the running of this ranch now, I never will be." His measured voice fell on his father's ears with almost a physical force, and Simon Meade's eyes widened with surprise. But before the older man could speak he said, "I'll put it plain. Either let Sun Ranch alone and get rid of Jack Bronte—or I'm out!"

Simon Meade stared at his son, unable to believe what he was hearing. "You can't do that, Lew! Who else have I built this ranch up for if not for you?"

"It's for me? Then let it be for me. You've said you want us to run this place together, but you won't listen to anything I say. I don't want to wait until you die before I start having a say in the ranch! We can work together! But not if we're going to become outlaws. I won't stand for that."

Perhaps it was guilt, or maybe shame, but whatever it was, his son's words brought a blind rage to Simon Meade. He snarled, "Get out then! Get out! See how hard it is to make a living for yourself! Go on!"

"Mean that, Dad?" Lew asked softly, his eyes fixed on the fierce face of his father.

"Yes, I mean it! Get out of here! You're no son of mine!"

Lew did not hesitate one moment. He turned and walked away to his bedroom. Simon Meade stood there, stunned. A few minutes later Lew came out with his gear stuffed in a bag and stopped long enough to say good-bye. "I hate to leave like this. I never expected it to come—but I can't go on living like this." He left the house, and a few moments later Simon Meade heard his son's horse as he rode out.

"He'll come back," Simon said aloud, defiantly. "He'll find out how tough it is out there, and he'll come draggin' back. Then maybe he'll listen to reason." Yet even as he spoke the confident words, there was a heaviness in him that he had never felt, and he knew that he was all alone in this empire that he had built, and there was no one to share it with.

He thought of his wife slaughtered and his baby boy stolen by the Sioux so many years ago, and the memory brought a sharp pain as it always did. Suddenly he had a vision of his wife's face—gentle and beautiful as it had been the day she left him. "You and Lew have a good time," she'd whispered. "I love you so much!" And then she'd stepped into the stage and ridden out of his life. *She wouldn't like all this,* he thought, then blotted out the memory.

Riding up out of one of the dry riverbeds carved out of the plain, Mona Reynolds was surprised to see in the distance a man up on top of an old shack that had long been abandoned. She pulled her horse up and strained her eyes but could not make out who it was. She had grown more cautious about riding away from Sun Ranch and now wore a small .38. Curiosity got the better of her, however, and she spurred her mare forward at a fast trot. When she got a hundred yards away, surprise ran over her when she saw it was Lew Meade.

She pulled up in front of him and looked up at him inquisitively. The mallet in his hands looked almost as out of place as a woman's bonnet would have! "Hello, Lew," she said. Her eyes swept the small shack, the poorly mended corral fences, and the run-down barn, then looked back at him. "What're you doing in this old place? Deacon told me it's been abandoned a long time."

Lew Meade had stripped his shirt off. Sweat ran down his face and chest. He was wearing a gray hat, and he pushed it back, grinning down at her crookedly. "Well, I guess you might say I'm launching my new profession." He walked across the roof to the ladder and climbed down, saying ruefully, "I picked a pretty slow way to get rich, don't you reckon?"

Mona stared at him, conscious of his lean, tall body as he lounged carelessly against a wall. His muscles were taut and defined, and he looked strong and fit. "What are you talking about?" she demanded. "What are you doing out here, Lew?"

"Well, get down and let's have a drink of water over at the spring, and I'll tell you about it." He waited until she dismounted and tied her horse to the rail of the corral he had recently—and clumsily—repaired, and then he led her over to where a small spring bubbled up out of a cleft in some rocks. He picked up a tin cup, filled it with the clear water, and handed it to her. As she drank, he said dryly, "That's about the only good thing about this spread. Got the best water in the territory, I think." He took the cup, refilled it, and drank with obvious enjoyment. Putting the cup back in a convenient hollow in a rock, he grew sober. "I guess you haven't heard, but my dad and I split the blanket."

"Split a blanket? What does that mean?" she asked in confusion.

He laughed then and said, "Split *the* blanket. Old Indian saying. When an Indian and his friend or his woman separate, they 'split the blanket.' It means they go their separate ways."

Mona could not believe what she was hearing. "What— what do you mean? You and your father quarreled?"

"Might call it that." Lew studied her, wanting to say more, but he knew it would sound odd coming from him. So he just went on casually, "Let's just say I'm a young fella launching out, trying to get his own ranch. C'mon, I'll show you around."

There wasn't much to see. He took her inside the shack,

which was only one room filled with patched-up furniture, a single bed, a cast-iron cookstove, and a beat-up table and two chairs. In some spots Mona could look up through large holes in the roof and see the broad Wyoming sky. "All the comforts of home," he said cheerfully. "Just a matter of time till it'll be New Castle in Bear Valley." He looked at the remnants of a meal still on the table and grinned. "First time I ever tried cooking. I don't know whether my stomach or my hands will wear out first." He held his hands out, and Mona saw huge blisters; some had been broken, and a few were even tinged with blood.

"Oh, Lew! That's terrible!" she gasped. "You can't work with your hands like that! Don't you have anything to tie around them?"

"I don't think so," he said carelessly. "They'd just blister up again anyhow."

"No, wait, I've got something in my saddlebags that'll do. Come on outside." She led him outside, rummaged in her saddlebags, and pulled out a pale blue cotton blouse. "Here. Let me have your knife," she ordered.

"Wait a minute, you're not going to ruin that good blouse!" he protested.

"I can only wear one blouse at a time," she answered matter-of-factly. "And your hands need it worse than I do." Using the knife, she cut the blouse into bandages and insisted that he bring some lard from the kitchen.

Lew stood looking down at her. As Mona held his hand and gently put the lard on his broken palms and wound the bandages around them, he said, "Good thing to have a nurse around. I guess I need a keeper, anyway." Then he added, "A pretty one, too."

Mona was used to receiving compliments, but the intimacy of holding his hands and tending to them made her flush. She smiled up at him and said, "You just lay off fence building and roof mending for a day and let these heal up."

"You're the doctor," he said with alacrity. "But on the condition that you stick around and help me fix something good to eat. I've got plenty of grub, but I can't cook worth a lick."

"All right," she answered, "I'll do it. Now lead me to the groceries."

The afternoon was reaching an end by the time they sat down to the meal that she had cooked, which really wouldn't have taken any prizes. "Deacon Boone would laugh at this," she said ruefully, "but I'm learning. He's a strange man, but one of the best cooks I've ever seen. Why, I think he could work in a fancy restaurant in Chicago! But he never will."

Lew ate heartily, and when he finished, he shoved back from the table and said, "That's the best meal I've had in two weeks, since I've been on this scrubby place. Come on, it's cooled off now. Let's walk down by the creek."

She followed Lew outside, and for the next half hour they strolled along the edge of a creek that touched the property and turned in an elbow that led back to the river. It was a pleasant little creek. From time to time birds gathered at it, and he pointed out the tracks of animals that had come to drink. The air grew cooler, and Mona said finally, "I've got to get back, Lew. It's going to be dark pretty soon."

"I guess so." He stopped, and they faced each other for a moment. "Going to be more lonesome after you leave," he said.

"What's this all about, Lew? What are you doing out here in that shack, anyway? You're not serious about living here—I mean, actually ranching, are you? You'll patch it up with your father—" A thought struck her, and she said with sudden realization, "Wait a minute! Did you quarrel with your father over Sun Ranch?"

Lew Meade thought for a moment and then nodded. "Well, that was the way of it, Mona. I told you before I don't agree with Dad. It got so bad I finally couldn't stand it, so I pulled out." He gestured awkwardly with one bandaged hand and said, "I really don't know what to do with myself. I've had it pretty easy all my life. Spoiled rotten, I expect. Son of one of the richest men in the valley."

Mona's face changed in the twilight, and she laughed suddenly. "Me, too," she said. "I grew up having everything I wanted. It's just since I've been at Sun that I've learned to appreciate something you do for yourself. Like that meal back there—I never cooked in my life and didn't really appreciate food, but now I can see what it's like when you have to do your own. You know," she added tentatively, "I really kind of like it, Lew."

"Do you?" he asked eagerly. "Then you understand what it's like. Oh, I know I'll never be rich, but this place could be made into a nice little ranch. Never be anything big, not even big as Sun, but I have a few cattle of my own, and if I can get this ranch together and get a couple of boys to come out and help me, why, we could feed out some young beef and supply some of the bigger ranches with feeding stock! That's what I'd like to do!"

The two of them talked animatedly while they continued their walk back. She was amused and yet touched at how he had thrown his easy life away and now spoke with such enthusiasm and excitement of starting over here. It was intriguing. Finally she said regretfully, "I've got to go."

Full dark was coming on quickly across the mountains,

sliding across the narrow valley, and the outlines of the hills were a black, ragged-edged mass against the glittering shine of a few high stars. A new moon tipped over on one of its horns and made a lightness on the low horizon. The heat that had pulsed upon the earth all day, thick-scented with dust and sage, was beginning to fade away.

In that moment of quietness Lew Meade felt the pull of Mona's beauty and put his hand on her arm. He saw her eyes widen and her lips open. In that one moment he had forgotten about Slash A and Sun Ranch and everything else. He took her into his arms, his mouth bearing down hard and heavy upon hers. He knew that her wishes joined with his, and he felt her give herself to him completely, then she pulled away with a slight gasp.

"I—I've got to go, Lew," she said a little breathlessly. She turned and walked away rapidly, wondering at herself. She was not a girl to give herself easily, and though she had been kissed before, somehow Lew Meade's touch had stirred her unlike any other man's. When they reached the yard, he untied her horse and held him as she mounted, then handed her the reins.

"I'm sorry," he said quietly, then went on abruptly, "No. That's not so. I'm not a mite sorry! You're a beautiful woman, Mona—more beautiful than any I've seen."

Mona looked down at his lean face that had grown completely serious. There was fun in him, she knew, but now he was looking at her in a way she did not quite understand. Taking a deep breath, she said, "Let's not drag this out, Lew. Sun and Slash A are headed for a war, and you know it." He started to speak, but she continued in a determined tone, "I know you've left your ranch, but what if one of our men killed your father? It would always be between us." She reached out her hand, and he took it. She squeezed his hand hard and said, "Thank you for showing me your place. I think it's wonderful, and I wish you well with it." She pulled her hand back, wheeled her horse, and rode away into the growing darkness.

Lew Meade stood quietly watching her, but his mind was not quiet. He had been shaken by her touch and knew that he would not be able to forget the feel of her lips on his or her body pressed against him.

★ ★ ★

Jack Bronte had not survived a hard life by being a fool. He had learned to read men well, and as he stood looking at Bax LeFarge, he thought he had the Slash A foreman pretty well figured out. LeFarge had come riding into the pocket and had been intercepted by one of Bronte's men, who had led him through the twisted canyons and scrub timber to the house beside a small stream, hidden in a canyon. It was not an impressive house, but Bronte was content. His day would come, and the pocket was his ticket to making a killing.

"Little surprised to see you here, Bax," he said easily. His dark eyes were fixed on LeFarge, and he waved at the bottle on the table. "Have a drink. That's a pretty thirsty ride all the way in from Slash A."

"You're right about that," LeFarge agreed, nodding. He looked huge in the small kitchen of the cabin where the two men sat. He poured a drink, looked at the amber shine of the liquor, and tossed it off, bracing his feet on the floor against the shock. Putting the glass down, he licked his lips and said, "So you didn't expect me, Jack?"

"Nope. I thought I'd settled everything with Meade last time we talked."

LeFarge shifted uneasily, the huge muscles of his shoulders bunching under his shirt. He poured another drink, downed it, then slammed the glass down. "You heard about Lew pullin' out?" When Bronte shook his head, LeFarge gave the outline of what had happened. Then he said, "The old man's not gonna make it, Jack. He ain't as tough as he used to be. He's gettin' soft, and Lew never was any good. He's a playboy, and I never knew a playboy that was worth a dime in a fight."

Jack Bronte nodded slightly. He was interested, as he was interested in everything that happened in Bear Valley. Leaning forward, he poured his own drink, sipped it carefully, and asked, "Well, what does that spell, Bax? What's in it for you?" He grinned slightly, saying, "You wouldn't be here if it wasn't about money, would you?"

"You know me," LeFarge said defiantly, "and I know you, Jack. We're both in this for all we can get. But it's not working out like I thought it would." He considered Bronte carefully, then went on, "On the other hand, it might work out even better."

"You're not gonna get your hands on Slash A." Jack shrugged. "Meade's too smart for that; he'll have it all tied up. And even if Lew ain't there to get it, somebody else will."

LeFarge nodded. "Yeah, somebody. But most of his ranch is free graze. He's just like Sun—he couldn't claim all of it. Maybe a thousand acres he owns title to. But there's another twenty thousand acres out there he controls, and *that's* the part I'm interested in." He looked across the table, his eyes glowing by the light of the lantern. "It's what you're interested in, too, ain't it, Jack?" He leaned back in his chair and said smugly, "You got ambition. I seen that a long time ago. You ain't gonna be satisfied forever up here in the pocket, pickin' off a few head here and there and sellin' 'em."

Bronte grinned, his teeth very white against his dark face. "Man that doesn't have any ambition's not worth much. What you got on your mind, Bax?"

LeFarge leaned forward and began to talk rapidly. "The way I see it, we've got to bust up Sun and Slash A. Get 'em to fightin' each other. Let 'em kill each other off! Then when the smoke clears, somebody's gonna step in and claim that free range. Even if we have to let the Reynolds woman have the owned part of Sun and let Meade perch on his thousand acres, there's still plenty of room for a big ranch in there. And I see myself ownin' a big chunk of it."

"And you need me, is that it, Bax?"

"We need each other," LeFarge said. "I control the crew at Slash A. You got your boys here. All we have to do is get a nice little war started and let the two shoot each other up. Wouldn't be long 'fore we could step in and take over."

Bronte understood that he would be of use to Bax LeFarge only as long as LeFarge needed him. He thought rapidly, *He'll do me in if he gets a chance. But then I'd do him in, too. So we'll see who winds up with that big ranch in the valley.* He nodded at Bax and said, "What you got on your mind, Bax? I'm with you."

He listened as LeFarge began to outline the plan. The two men sat there for a long time. Finally LeFarge stood up and said, "OK, we've got a deal. You've got it all straight?"

"Sure," Bronte said readily, and got to his feet, sleek and lithe, looking like a huge cat. He smiled pleasantly and poured two drinks. Handing one to Bax, he said, "Here's to a new partnership." The two men downed the drinks, and LeFarge left.

Bronte began to pace the room, his fertile mind active. After a few minutes he ran to the door and called out, "Vinnie! George! Get the boys in here! We got a little chore comin' up!"

# FIFTEEN
## The War Begins

Deacon Boone peered critically at the pie crust that Belle Montez had produced, touched it with an experimental finger, then nodded. "Well, now, Miss Belle, I reckon I ain't such a bad teacher after all." His blue eyes gleamed with humor as he added, "Here it's taken me nigh onto fifty years to learn how to make a pie—and you learnt it in one morning!"

Belle Montez was wearing a simple blue dress, and her arms were covered with flour. She smiled at Boone, but there was a wistful look in her eye when she answered, "I guess I never had time to learn to cook, Deacon."

"Your ma never taught you that?"

"I never really knew my mother. She died when I was three, and my father died when I was eight. I was passed around among the relatives until I was sixteen, and then I had to go to work." She took the pie crust from Deacon, walked back to the table, put it down, and began layering apple slices in it. "I went to work as a waitress, and then I got a job in a dance hall. Pretty soon I learned I could sing a little, and that made things a little bit easier. But it was still hard. Finally I fell in love. But before we could marry, he died in an accident."

Boone walked over to stand beside her. "That's enough apples. You don't want to get too much filler in it." He studied her carefully, then said gently, "Sounds like a tough life, Belle, working in a dance hall. I know it musta been hard on you."

Belle frowned down at the pie. She had completely recovered from her illness and had told Lillian Reynolds that she had to leave because she was a burden, but Lillian had merely said, "Oh, pooh, you can stay as long as you please. You keep me company." Belle had stayed, but had thrown herself into helping Deacon Boone do the cooking and some of the cleaning. She had learned to respect Boone. He was the first religious man she'd ever known who made religion part of his whole life. Carefully she had waited for him to say something or do something that would prove it was just talk. But now, after two weeks, she knew that his love for God was real.

"I never went to church after I was a child," she said slowly, still looking down. Painstakingly she began placing the dough in a lattice pattern that would form the top crust of the pie. Without intending to reveal herself, she continued idly, "I think I missed something. Everyone needs some religion."

Boone answered quickly, "Why, Belle, everybody's got religion of some kind. The heatherns worship the stars, and some people even worship trees, I hear." His voice filled with warm humor as he said, "Wouldn't that be somethin'! Gettin' down and prayin' to a persimmon tree!"

Belle looked up, a smile touching her lips. "Well, that's no worse than worshiping money, I guess. Or pleasure, like a lot of people do. I've seen them." She formed the top crust of the pie with care, held it up, and asked, "How's that?"

"Jest right! Now, let's stick that little hummer in the oven, and when them hollow-bellied riders get in, they'll have somethin' to sink their teeth into." She put the pie in the oven, and Deacon said, "Now let's make a coupla peach pies."

As the two began gathering the ingredients and making the dough, Belle asked curiously, "How is it you're so happy all the time, Deacon? You're not rich."

"Well," Boone said, "I guess I kind of am. The Bible says I'm a child of the King, and I never knowed of a poor king, did you?" He grinned at her but then grew sober. "You know, most men and women spend all their time trying to make things right on the outside. 'If I can just live in a big enough house,' they say, or 'If I can get enough horses or fine clothes or have enough money to travel, then I'll be happy.' And I tried that. Done pretty good too, Belle. Had me a good business and just about everything else. One day I went to the doctor, and he told me I wasn't goin' to live but a year."

"I never knew that, Deacon!"

"Well," he said, grinning, "that was eleven years ago, so doctors don't know everything. But it scairt me, I can tell you. I looked around at the big house I had, and the horses, and the fancy clothes, and my bank account. And all I could think of was, *This'll all be gone when I draw my last breath.* So I set out to find something more real than that, and it didn't take me no time to find out where it was. I guess the good Lord led me," he said softly, rolling the dough slowly in his stubby hands. "I went to a revival meetin' and heard a preacher. Never will forget that. Preached on John 3, 'Ye Must Be Born Again.' You know that Scripture, Miss Belle?"

"I don't think so."

"Here. You do this dough, and I'll set back and read it to

you. I always did like to rest and watch a woman work." He washed his hands at the pump, reached up to a shelf over the sink, and pulled out a worn Bible.

"This here chapter," he said with a warm light in his faded blue eyes, "tells about a fella that had all the religion a man needs. Name of Nicodemus. He come to Jesus one time after dark, and I dunno what he expected, but he sure got both barrels when Jesus turned loose on him! Here, let me read it to you. It says here: 'There was a man of the Pharisees, named Nicodemus, a ruler of the Jews: The same came to Jesus by night, and said unto him, Rabbi, we know that thou art a teacher come from God: for no man can do these miracles that thou doest, except God be with him. Jesus answered and said unto him, Verily, verily, I say unto thee, Except a man be born again, he cannot see the kingdom of God. Nicodemus saith unto him, How can a man be born when he is old? can he enter the second time into his mother's womb, and be born? Jesus answered, Verily, verily, I say unto thee, Except a man be born of water and of the Spirit, he cannot enter into the kingdom of God. That which is born of the flesh is flesh; and that which is born of the Spirit is spirit.'

"That there's what got me. 'That which is born of the flesh is flesh; and that which is born of the Spirit is spirit.'"

He paused, and Belle looked at him with a puzzled expression. "I don't understand, Deacon. What does it mean?"

"Well, it just means all of us got two parts, Belle. Flesh and spirit. And like I said, I was spendin' all my time on the flesh—houses, horses, and money. But there's another part of me that wasn't doin' nothin', and that was the spirit. That part inside." He looked at her with a kindly expression and said, "You've got a spirit, Belle. I know you've had a hard life, but

I've seen there's a goodness and a sweetness that's just tryin' to get out."

Belle flushed and suddenly recognized that here was only the second man she'd ever known—the first being Jim Reno— that had seen beneath her exterior. "Thank you, Deacon," she said softly. "I wish that were true, but I can't seem to break away."

"Sure, all of us got that trouble," Deacon assured her. "It wasn't hard for me 'cause it was life or death. But for most folks, they keep on tryin' to do somethin' in the flesh when all the time Jesus wants to do somethin' in the spirit. Lemme tell you 'bout how I got saved."

He went on to relate his conversion experience as Belle worked on the pies. For over an hour the two talked. When the pies were in the oven, she asked, "But how does one get born again?"

"That's just what Nicodemus asked, ain't it, Belle? Well, I don't think anybody could explain that, no more'n you could explain how a child comes into bein'. All you know is some of the particulars, but birth is always a miracle. Every single birth! But here's what the Bible says. Over in the book of Acts in the sixteenth chapter a fella came in and asked the apostle Paul, 'What must I do to be saved?' Then in verse thirty-one, 'And they said, Believe on the Lord Jesus Christ, and thou shalt be saved, and thy house.'"

"But I believe in God," Belle said in a puzzled tone. "I haven't obeyed him or served him—but I've always believed in God."

"Sure, me too. But this is different, Belle. When a person gets saved it's like gettin' married. The Bible talks about it like that. If you ever get married, you'll stand up beside some man, and you'll give him your hand, and you'll give him your heart and your mind and your body, and your whole life, ain't that so?"

Belle nodded. "That's so."

"Well, that's what I done. I called on Jesus, and I gave him everything I had. And you know what, Belle?" Tears gathered in Boone's wise old eyes, and he almost whispered, "Right there, right then, when I called on Jesus, somethin' happened to me. Nobody coulda told it on the outside, but inside I was different. I just knowed that God was inside of me—that Jesus had come. And ever since that day," he said, and here he took out a red bandanna and wiped his eyes, "ever' mornin' when I get up, I just say, 'Thank you, Jesus, for comin' into my life and for stayin' with me and for lovin' me and for takin' care of me.' And then I tell him I'm lookin' for the day that I'll be with him. And that's my religion in a nutshell."

Belle was touched by his emotion and felt her own eyes growing a little misty. She ducked her head and said almost under her breath, "I'd give anything if I could live like that, Deacon." She looked up then, a troubled expression on her beautiful face. "Do you think Jesus would come into my life if I'd ask him?"

"You bet! 'Him that cometh to me I will in no wise cast out,' the Scripture says." He smiled at her and said, "Belle, why don't you do it right now? I mean—why, ain't no better time than the present." Then he added, "I know you got lotsa troubles. And I know you're a young woman, got a lot of life ahead of you, prob'ly. But you can live it better with Jesus in you than any other way."

Belle had never been swept by such feelings. She longed to find a peace like Deacon spoke of. She sighed and said, "All right. I've tried everything else, Deacon. Will you pray for me?"

"Sure I will. You just bow your head, and we'll go tell God about all this." He bowed his head, Belle bowed hers, and there was a quietness in the room. She had half expected that Deacon would start praying at the top of his lungs like she had heard some preachers do, but when he finally spoke, it was just as if he spoke to her or to one of his friends.

"Lord Jesus," he said, "this here is your child. I'm askin' you to come into Belle's heart and to make her fresh and new as a little baby. Take away ever' wrong thing that she ever done and put it under the blood. Let her know that you're there and from now on let her be a child of God and on her way to heaven." He said no more, but he leaned over and put his hand over hers, and they sat there quietly. Finally he said, "Belle, you just tell Jesus who you are, what you've done, and that you want somethin' new, that you want him in your life."

Belle obeyed, hardly knowing what she was saying. Finally when she finished, she looked up at Deacon, her eyes overflowing with tears. "Well, I asked him, Deacon. Do you think he's come?"

"I *know* he has, if you asked him," Deacon said with a warm smile. "Now, lemme go through some of these Scriptures and tell you how a baby has to learn to live a brand-new kinda life. Jesus is gonna be with you, but you got a lot to learn, Belle. If you'll let me, I'll sure be glad to help you."

The two of them talked in the quiet kitchen for a long time, and when Belle finally got up and went outside to walk in the late morning air, she somehow knew that things would never be the same again. There was a peace in her heart and a certainty that she would never again be burdened down over her life. She began to hum as she walked along, thinking of the morning's events.

★ ★ ★

Belle said nothing about her conversion to anyone. She kept to herself for the next three days, going to bed early, reading for hours in the Bible that she'd found in Lillian Reynolds' small bookcase. She had quickly discovered that she knew nothing about being a Christian, and she spent so much time with Deacon that Lillian began to be a little bit suspicious.

"Deacon loves to talk about religion, doesn't he," Lillian said one day to Belle. "He's such a good man, too—he means every word of it." She stared at the young woman and said, "You've been very quiet, Belle. Is anything wrong?"

Belle smiled, saying, "No, Lillian. It's just that I've been thinking about my life, and Deacon's helped me to see some things."

Lillian said carefully, "I haven't wanted to ask, Belle, but everyone knows you came out to marry Dave Holly. Do you think that will ever happen?"

"I don't know, Lillian." Belle's face was composed. "He's a good man." She paused and gave Lillian a straight look. "I haven't led a good life. You know that, and Dave does, too. I'm not sure he could ever forget it—he or any other man."

Lillian's brown eyes glowed with affection. "Don't say that, Belle. Anyone can change, and if Dave is a good man, he'll take you just as you are."

Later that morning Dave Holly came riding in. He had been visiting the ranch often but had recently been away on a drive to Cheyenne. When he came in, there was an eagerness in his eyes as he met Belle. He took her hand, saying, "I've missed you, Belle. And you're looking good, like brand-new! How do you feel?"

"Fine, Dave. How did your business in Cheyenne go?"

"I got the best deals for my cattle since I've been out here. Let me tell you about it." He sat down at the table and spoke rapidly, eyes glowing as he related his trip. When he finished he said, "I made enough, I think, to get the house fixed up, do some things I needed to do." He paused then and a soberness fell on him. It was not sadness, exactly, but there was a look of doubt in his eye. "I made a mistake about us, Belle. I should've married you the day you came to town."

His honesty, as always, touched Belle, and she said, "We all make mistakes, Dave. But sometimes we can get over them."

He seized her words and stood up, pulling her close. "That's what I came to ask you, Belle. Let's forget everything else. Let's ride into town right now and get married." He was not a man of words, and neither was he a man who showed affection easily. He went on awkwardly, "I love you, Belle, is what I'm trying to say, and I want to marry you and have you for my wife."

"Oh, Dave," Belle said, her eyes disturbed, "I can't make a decision right now. We'll have to wait awhile."

Disappointment came into his eyes, and he said dispiritedly, "I don't blame you. I'm not much for a woman like you, beautiful and all."

"It's not that," she said quickly. Then she made a helpless little gesture and looked at him pleadingly. "Dave, you know what I've been. I haven't led a good life. I worked in a saloon, wandered around all over the country. . . ." Her voice broke a little, and she swallowed hard. "And I've known men, too. I couldn't hide that from you—you know it already." She turned and walked to the window and stared out blindly. "That would be hard for a man to forget."

"I'd forget it," he said firmly. He came to stand behind her, put his hands on her arms, and turned her around. "I promise, Belle, I'd never say a word. Never."

"But I'm afraid you would remember, and it would come between us." She drew back a little and said, "Besides, I have to tell you one more thing, Dave. Since I've been here, I've been talking to Deacon a lot. He's a man of God, you know, a real one. And I've decided that the only way I'll ever be able to have anything is to live for God. So I gave him my life, Dave. And whatever comes, I'm going to follow Jesus Christ."

He stared at her, unable to speak for a moment. Then a thoughtful look came into his hazel eyes, and he said, "My mother was a Christian. The finest one I ever knew. She died when I was sixteen. And the last thing she said was, 'Dave, I want you to follow Jesus, and find a woman who loves Jesus, and make a life.' That was the last thing she said. And I ain't never forgot it."

"Are you a Christian then, Dave?" Belle asked quietly.

"No, I ain't," he answered honestly. "But I need to be. Every man does. And I've put it off too long. You reckon Deacon would help me a little bit?"

"Oh, yes, Dave, I'm sure he would. But I'm still not sure about us. We'll just have to wait."

Suddenly a smile pulled at the corners of Dave Holly's mouth. "Somehow I got the idea that it's gonna happen. But I won't be pestering you, Belle. I'll be hanging around, and talking to Deacon a lot, and to you, too. I ain't much to look at, but

I'm stubborn as a mule. So you'll just have to get used to me bein' around, I guess."

Belle smiled sweetly and said, "That won't be too hard to do, Dave. Come on now, come with me down to the barn. I want to show you the new calf."

★  ★  ★

Holly left early with a promise to return soon. Later that afternoon Belle saw Reno getting ready to ride out. She hurried across the yard and called, "Jim, can I talk to you?"

"Why, sure. I'm just getting ready to go down to pull in a few of the weaker head of stock. You want to ride along? You feel up to it?"

"Of course," she answered eagerly. She had ridden several times on one of the gentler horses that either Chris or Reno had saddled for her. She hurried to change into riding clothes while Jim saddled her horse. When she ran back out, he was holding the reins of a sweet-tempered mare. He helped her up into the saddle, then mounted his horse.

"Come on," he said, "let's see if you can take a trot." They rode out, headed for the short hills to the east. The air seemed to grow cooler as they went through the pine timber. Finally he slowed the pace, saying, "That's enough of that, I guess." He looked at her with approval. "You sure do look good, Belle. I can't believe you've come along so fast. Got your color back and everything."

"It's been a wonderful time for me, Jim," she said. "The best I've ever known. Lillian is such a wonderful woman, like the mother I never had."

"She sure is. The whole family's fine people."

They rode along in silence and seeming tranquility, but

Belle noticed that Jim Reno's eyes were never still, that he was always looking from point to point, not missing a thing. "Are you expecting trouble, Jim?" she asked quietly.

"Always trouble around." His face looked very tan in the late afternoon sun, and his hands were brown as he held the reins lightly. He was strong, a quality in men she had always admired and oftentimes feared. But with Reno she experienced no fear, only confidence. Now he casually changed the subject. "Have you made up your mind about anything, Belle?"

She knew he meant Dave Holly. "Dave wants me to marry him," she said, "but I'm not sure that I can."

"Why not? He's a good man. A little hotheaded," Jim admitted with a sly grin, "but I think he plunged into me because he thinks so much of you."

"It's not that, I've got a temper myself. But there are two things that stand in the way. First is my past. I can't change that." He tried to speak, but she hurriedly went on. "Maybe Dave could forget that, but—I've been wanting to tell you, Jim. Something happened to me three days ago. . . ." She related her conversation with Deacon and her decision to become a Christian. She ended by saying, "I don't know how I'm going to do it, but I know I've got to serve God. And Dave isn't a Christian. Deacon told me that the most important thing for a woman to do is find a good Christian husband. If she didn't, her life would be hard."

Reno took all this in, then nodded in agreement. "You know, I think Deacon's right. I remember the Bible says, 'Can two walk together, except they be agreed?'" He turned to face her, and his eyes were warm with appreciation. "But I'm glad for you. Some of my people were fine Christians, and I've known others. So if you're going on to serve God, then God's on your side."

Belle's face glowed and her lips grew soft. "Thanks, Jim. I needed to hear that."

The two rode along, following a beaten trail. Finally Jim said, "There they are," indicating a dozen or so cattle grazing in an open valley. "Time to play cowboy, I guess. Wanna help me drive them back?"

"All right." Belle's eyes sparkled.

They rode toward the herd, Reno swinging around behind the cattle. He waited until Belle circled and came to the other side of the small herd. He called out, "Now, here we—"

At that moment a shot broke the stillness of the evening air, and Reno heard the slug strike the ground at his feet. "Belle! Belle! Ride out of here!" he yelled. He spurred his horse, riding to get between the woman and the timber when another rifle opened up. This time, he knew, they were shooting at Belle. "It's a woman, you fools!" he yelled, but the only answer was a fusillade of shots.

He pulled his gun and waited until he saw the wink of a rifle in the sun, then laid a shot on it. When he reached Belle, he said evenly, "We can't make it across open ground. Make for the timber." He maneuvered his horse, grabbed her bridle, and the two of them plunged into a thicket. Just as they entered the timber he heard Belle cry out and looked back to see her sway in the saddle. At the same time his horse grunted and stumbled. He kicked his feet free and jumped as the horse fell to the ground. They had reached the edge of the timber, and Belle's horse plunged on ahead. Snatching the rifle from the boot of his saddle, he dodged and ran after the panicked mare.

The bushes clawed at his face, and he heard the horse

slowing down, farther on. Behind him he heard men yelling, "Get 'em! Get 'em! They've gone into the timber." He was sure he recognized the rough voice of Bax LeFarge, and he thought bitterly, *They picked a fine time to start this war. With a woman, no less.*

He kept fighting his way through the thick underbrush and found the horse standing in a small clearing. Belle was still in the saddle, leaning forward. "Are you hit bad?" Reno asked hoarsely, leaning up to try to see.

"No—I—I don't think so," she said faintly. She held out her arm, and he saw that the upper part of her sleeve was bloody. Quickly he ripped the sleeve back and saw with relief that the bullet had missed the bone, but the wound was bleeding freely. Whipping off his neckerchief, he deftly bandaged her and said, "Come on, we've got to get out of here. They'll be after us. Can you hang on?"

"Yes."

He grabbed the bridle and led the horse deeper into the woods. Once he heard the pursuers, and he said, "Belle, I've got to leave you here for a minute. I'm gonna slow them down."

"Be careful, Jim," she said calmly. "I'll be all right. It only hurts a little."

He picked up his rifle, then dodged back through the woods, stopping from time to time to listen. There was a thrashing over to his left, and he moved silently that way. The light was fading fast, but he saw glimpses of horsemen coming through the brush. Stepping behind a tall pine tree, he levered a shell into the chamber and raised the rifle. Taking quick aim, he pulled the trigger and saw a man throw his arms high and fall out of his saddle. He levered another chamber and started laying down a withering fire on the horsemen.

The men following couldn't stand it. Reno briefly paused his firing to reload. One of the men cried, "He's got us! Let's get outta here! Pick Baldy up! Let's go!" And amidst all the confusion Jim's ears picked up another voice that said, "Baldy's a dead one—right through the heart."

Jim's lips tightened, but he resumed his steady firing. The horsemen drew back, and he turned and ran back to Belle. "We've got to get out of here. We'll circle around and get back to the ranch."

"What's happening, Jim? Why did they shoot at us?" Belle asked in bewilderment.

"I guess," he said, "the war has begun."

"Where's your horse?" Belle asked as Reno led her mount through the forest.

"Got shot when you did, only he didn't fare as well." As they worked their way he said, "I hope we get back to the ranch before they hit it."

He knew that a range war meant no quarter asked or given. As soon as they were clear of the timber, he swung up behind Belle and pushed the horse as fast as it could travel, back toward Sun Ranch.

# SIXTEEN
## *In the Short Hills*

Easy and Lee were sitting on the front porch, watching the sun go down over the edges of the mountains. Easy said, "Boy, can you smell that pie? My stomach thinks my throat's been cut! Why, I recollect one time when I was a yonker, back home—" He broke off suddenly and got to his feet. "Hoss comin', in a big hurry," he remarked tersely. He stepped down and walked out into the yard with Lee following him. The Reynoldses were getting ready for supper, and the riders were all in the bunkhouse.

Easy peered at the horse that appeared at the end of the meadow and said, "Got two riders. Somethin's wrong, Lee." He moved forward into the yard and waited, Lee coming to stand beside him. "That's Jim and Belle," Easy murmured.

Reno pulled the jaded animal to a stop, slipped off, and began to help Belle down, saying with no preface, "Roust the hands out, Easy."

"Trouble?" Easy Jones asked, his eyes growing bright. "I'll get them boys."

He ran off into the growing darkness, and Lee asked,

"What's the matter? Are you hurt, Miss Belle?" Jim was easing her from the saddle gently, and she winced slightly as her feet hit the ground. Lee saw the bloody sleeve, and his eyes grew wide. "What happened?"

"We got ambushed in the hills. Come on, Belle, we'll get Lillian to put a decent bandage on that arm."

The two walked across the yard, Lee following, and when they stepped inside Lillian met them. She saw Belle's pale face and bloody arm and said at once, "Here, we'll have to wash that out. What happened, Jim?"

"Somebody opened up on us, Lillian. Can you take care of Belle?"

"Of course."

By this time Chris and Mona had come in and were staring at the scene before them. Reno said, "We can't stay here. The ranch is going to be raided. Get Belle's arm bandaged as quick as you can, Lillian."

He wheeled and walked out, followed by Chris, while the two women attended to Belle's wound. They met Pack Ganton and the rest of the crew, who had followed Easy back.

"What's going on?" Ganton demanded.

"Got hit in the hills," Reno said briefly. "They'll be coming this way pretty quick. They tried to pick us off, but I think they were hopin' to ambush the ranch."

"Who was it, Jim?" Ollie Dell asked, his eyes glittering.

"I thought I heard Bax LeFarge, so it must be Slash A." Jim's mouth set in an even tighter line, and he went on grimly, "I don't know what set 'em off, but they're coming. Go get your rifles and plenty of ammunition. We can't hold this ranch— Slash A has us outnumbered."

"We can hold it," Chris said defiantly. "They can't run us

off from here." He ran back toward the house to get his gun, and the crew dispersed.

Easy told Jim, "I dunno. They can take potshots at us from those trees any time they take a notion. Maybe we ort to ride out and meet 'em, Jim. Do a little ambushin' ourself."

Reno shook his head. "We've gotta get those women out of here. Somebody's gotta take them to town."

"That leaves us with one less man," Lee pointed out. He assumed that Jim would assign him the job since he was the youngest, and he was right.

"Lee, get the wagon hitched up. Take the women out of here as quick as you can." He saw a protest forming on the boy's lips, and he quickly went on, "Lee, it'll have to be this way. Somebody's gotta look out for the women."

Lee sighed, then said, "OK, Jim. I'll get the wagon hitched."

He ran toward the barn, and Jim turned to Easy, saying grimly, "We can't hold this place."

"What are you gonna do, Jim?"

"I think we'll have to pull out, head for the hills. If we do that, they'll have to follow us, and we can hold 'em off with a rear guard. C'mon, let's get ready to pull out of here."

Lee was bringing the wagon out while Jim went inside to confront the women. "I'm sending you to town," he said. "Lee will take you."

"I don't want to leave here," Mona said stubbornly. In the short time she had been on the ranch, she had become a different young lady. The ranch had come to mean something—a home, an anchor, someplace to belong to. She squared her shoulders, eyes flashing, and said, "I can shoot. We can hold out here."

"No. We can't risk it. Come on."

A protest leaped to Mona's lips, but Lillian said, "Jim's right. We'd just be in the way. Come along, Belle."

They went outside, where the night breeze was beginning to run through the trees, with its blend of dust and grass and pine. Reno stood motionless for a moment; the night silence had an edge of suspense. The crew was around him, waiting, the tension building.

Pack Ganton said, "Well, what are we—"

"Quiet! Listen!" Reno snapped. He took one step toward the backyard and stopped. Things were turning wrong while he delayed. He made a circle, staring into the increasing blackness of the trees. He listened hard, and his head lifted suddenly. Easy heard it also.

"Somethin's up!"

"You women, get into the wagon, now!"

"I don't want to go!" Mona argued.

"Now!" Reno barked. It grew worse and worse. He took one step, halted, then swung toward the backyard. Suddenly he broke into a run, toward the corral. "Come on! Come on! Lee, get those women out of here!" He reached the corral with the crew tumbling behind him. "Everyone, mount up!"

And then it came. Riders came down the hill and passed the house full tilt. They had circled around during the falling darkness to come down out of the hills. Pack Ganton cursed loudly. Ollie said, "Here they come!"

Jim called, "Wait, Lee! Bring that wagon over this way!"

And then they heard it. Simon Meade's voice calling out, "Left side of the house! Left side of the house!"

It was Easy who fired the first shot, and almost at once the rest of the crew were firing at the shadowy figures who circled to try to get behind the barn. Reno said, "Let's get out of here! That way, Lee!"

Lee's eyes followed Reno's gesture, then he snapped the traces and gave a loud sharp command to the horses. The wagon leaped forward, and the three women held on as it plunged out of the yard, careening over the uneven earth.

"Cover the wagon!" Jim called out. "Move out!" The crew formed an uneven, ragged line at the back of the wagon as the Slash A crew boiled into the backyard. The steady, hard-ground claps of gunfire broke into the trees and up on the flats and echoed on and on through the hillside. Reno knew that Meade had brought his whole crew, for the pressure of his out-fit was growing steadily worse. "Lay it on!" he yelled. Bullets clipped the trees near at hand, and he heard them sing and scatter.

"Wilson, you and Meeks stay here with me!" Jim called. "The rest of you pull out!" Wilson and Meeks appeared beside him. Meeks was reloading his gun, cursing steadily. The wagon pulled out with the rest of the crew. As soon as they disappeared into the darkness, Jim said, "Forget those six-guns. Pull your rifles." He drew the two men back as the shots sang shrilly around their ears. "Get on foot, hide the horses. We'll hold 'em off here until the wagon gets away."

Tuck Wilson and Patch Meeks did what he said. They tied their horses behind the spring house, then they came back and began to lay down a fire on the Slash A men. Still they heard yelling, and above all was Bax LeFarge's voice crying, "Ride 'em down! Ride 'em down!"

Jim and his two men held them off for a while, but the Slash A men were slowly circling to surround them. "We've gotta get out of here," Jim said, his jaw clenched. "Get mounted. They ought to be far enough away we can set up an ambush."

"All right, Reno," Wilson said. He turned to go to his horse and suddenly gasped, falling to his hands and knees, then he slumped and rolled over.

Jim called out, "Wilson!" and moved to roll him over, but he saw that the rider had taken a bullet in the temple. "Let's get out of here, Patch!" he yelled. The two men ran to the waiting horses, mounted, and rode away, bullets whistling all around them.

The smell of powder hung in the yard after the firing ceased. The Sun outfit had vanished. Lester Box prowled around in the darkness and came back to say, "We need to get after them, Mr. Meade. They're gonna get away."

Simon Meade stood, his white hair blowing in the wind as he took off his hat and wiped his forehead. He said shakily, "I thought you told me the women wouldn't be here, LeFarge."

LeFarge shrugged. "I heard they were all supposed to be in town. That was the word we got."

Box took a step closer to Simon Meade and said impatiently, "We gotta get after them. They're gonna get away. And if they get up into those hills, we ain't never gonna catch 'em."

"Lester's right," LeFarge said. "We gotta make a clean job out of it." He saw that Meade was shaken and said, "They'll send the women away, now that they're clear."

Meade stared at his foreman and said, "This thing could turn out bad." His eyes probed the growing darkness and he finally said, "We'll wait till the women are clear, then we'll run 'em down in the hills."

LeFarge didn't like this. "That won't do," he argued. "We've gotta get 'em now!" Then he went on in a more placating tone, "Tell you what. We'll catch up to 'em and give 'em a chance to turn the women loose for town."

Simon Meade didn't look at his foreman. He said in a low voice, "We never should have done this. Even if Sun was stealing our cattle." He had not believed it at first when LeFarge had come in with the report that Sun riders had taken a large herd from one of their lower pastures. But when he had ridden off and seen the tracks himself, he had to admit that it was true. Only then had LeFarge been able to convince him that the only path left to him was to make a raid on Sun and wipe them out. But LeFarge had assured him that the women would be in town.

Now he looked old and worn as he stood there, trying to think. Finally he said heavily, "Send a couple men out to scout for them, and leave a few here to make sure they don't come back. Everyone else will head back to Slash A and then head out in the morning when we have a better chance of spottin' them."

★ ★ ★

Holly looked up to see a rider coming at a hard gallop and pulled up his horse. Once the rider pulled up shortly in front of him, Holly said lazily, "What's the rush, Lew?"

Lew Meade's horse was lathered and heaving from the hard run he had made. Dust covered Lew's hat and sunburned face. He gasped, "Did you hear what happened at Sun?"

Holly grew immediately alert and straightened in the saddle. "What's the matter? What happened?"

It was hard for Lew, but he said grimly, "Slash A raided them last night."

"Anybody hurt?" Holly demanded.

"One of Sun's men got killed, and one of Slash A's boys got the same medicine." He studied Holly and said, "I don't know how you stand on all this, Dave. You haven't said much about it. But you know that Belle Montez was there."

Dave Holly slapped the reins against his saddle in an angry gesture. "I never thought your dad would be fool enough to do a thing like that! What's got into him? Sure, I knew he'd pressure Sun, but this is murder! And rustling, too!"

Lew sighed heavily and his face grew sad. "He's gone crazy, I think. Somehow it's got something to do with Jack Bronte. Wouldn't surprise me if him and LeFarge cooked up some scheme. I tried to get Dad to pull out of it, but he wouldn't listen." Then he clenched his jaw and, looking back up at Dave Holly with narrowed eyes, said, "I need a horse, Dave."

Holly studied him. "You going to find them?"

"Yes."

With no hesitation Holly said, "Come on, we'll get you a fresh mount. One for me, too."

His words surprised Lew Meade. "You'll be going up against Slash A, you know that, don't you? They can hit you just as well as they can Sun."

"I know that," Holly said grimly. He was angry clear through, Lew saw. Nothing else was said until they had saddled two fresh horses.

As they swung into the saddles, Holly asked, "How do we find them, Lew?"

"They're somewhere in the Short Hills. I got word from Charlie Cole, one of the hands that thinks my father's a fool for doing this. We've always been pretty close. He was in on the raid, but he wouldn't do any shooting. He came across their tracks going south last night, but he told LeFarge he couldn't track 'em down. He rode out to my place before dawn and filled me in. I figure they ought to be somewhere up around Dent's Canyon by this time. And they got the women with them in a wagon, so they can't run too fast or too far."

"You figure Slash A will go after 'em?" Holly asked tersely.

Lew's lips made a thin line. "Yeah. Cole said Dad was going to send most of the men out this morning."

"You'll go up against your father?" Holly was curious.

"If I have to. Come on, let's get out of here. They may be in trouble right now."

The two men rode hard, and by noon they were in the Short Hills. Both of them knew the country well and moved carefully, not wanting to encounter any of Slash A's men. From time to time they heard a rifle shot, long silences in between them. Lew said, "That's probably a signal. They're trying to surround the Sun crew. I know a way, though, that they probably don't. It's pretty hard going, but we can cut through and make it."

He led Holly into rough country, down some steep canyons, through some thickets, and the horses were exhausted by the time they came out into some foothills. "I think they might be over towards Crater Lake," Lew said. "It'd be a good place to hole up."

They proceeded as fast as possible on their tired animals and late in the afternoon crossed into some more foothills. They climbed steadily until finally they were stopped by a voice that said, "Hold it right there, you two!"

At once both men pulled up their horses, and Holly said, "It's Dave Holly and Lew Meade!"

Easy Jones stepped out from behind a tree, the rifle in his hands pointed casually toward them. "Howdy, fellers." His voice was cordial, but his eyes were sharp and the rifle didn't waver. "What can we do for ya?"

"Take us to Reno," Holly said. "We need to talk to him."

Easy stood motionless for a moment, eyes fixed on Lew. Then he said in the same tone, "All right." His eyes narrowed, and he went on, "Now you two fellers go on and just be easy how you move them hands. I'm a little bit nervous, you see."

The two riders nodded and gently touched their horses, and Easy followed them as they crossed a heavily wooded area.

They came out into a clearing, and Lew said, "There's Reno." His eyes moved over the clearing, and he said with relief, "It looks like Mrs. Reynolds and Mona are all right."

Holly had already spotted Belle and felt relief running through him with a force that he could not believe. He had been badly shaken by the news that Belle had been in danger, and it was clear to him how deep his feelings were for her.

The two men got off their horses as Reno came up. Holly said evenly, "Glad you got away, Reno. Lew just brought the news about the raid."

Reno asked him, "You sure you want to be here, Dave? It's gonna get pretty hot."

Holly said, "I came to take Belle out of this." Then he added, "I can take the other women if you want me to."

"They need to get out of here," Reno agreed. "I didn't want to risk them getting ambushed. But you can guard them well enough."

He turned to face Lew Meade, who was watching Mona, and said, "Bad place for you to be, Lew."

Lew Meade said deliberately, "I'm where I want to be," and walked over to Mona Reynolds.

She looked up, surprise evident on her face. "Lew! I didn't

think you'd come!" She said no more, but he read her thoughts.

"I know. But I've got to do this if I call myself a man. Are you all right? You and your mother?"

"Yes." She reached forward timidly and touched his arm. "I'm glad you came," she whispered. "We need all the help we can get. But you'll be going up against your own father."

He covered her small hand with his. "I'll be all right, but you and the other women have to get clear of this."

Holly had turned from Reno and gone to Belle. He stopped short when he saw her bandaged arm. "Belle, you've been hurt!"

"It's not serious," she said quickly. A warm light came to her eyes at his concern, and she said quietly, "It's good to see you here, Dave."

He held her hand for one moment, then said quickly, "If you and the other women will get ready, I'll take you out of here."

Belle said, "All right. I know we're just a burden on Jim now."

She turned to go, but he stopped her. When she turned to face him, he took a deep breath and said, "I nearly died when I heard you were up here, in the midst of all this. If anything had happened to you, well, I—I—"

She was touched by his words and smiled warmly. "Why, Dave, I didn't know you felt that strongly."

He looked a little embarrassed. He took her arm, awkwardly saying, "Come on, we can talk when everyone's safe."

Soon the three women were in the wagon leaving the hills, Holly driving the wagon in a circuitous route to avoid the Slash A riders. They rode all evening and far into the night before they were safely on the road that led to Banning. Belle said to Holly, "Dave, I want you to do something."

"Anything," he said instantly. "Just give me a chance to prove how I feel about you."

"I don't ask it because of that," Belle said quietly. "But Jim's in so much trouble. There's too many against him. Go back and help him. Please."

Holly stared at her in astonishment. "After I fought with him? I don't even know if he'd take my help." Then his face fell, and he said more honestly, "I've thought at times that you looked at him in a way—well—in a way I'd like to have you look at me."

"I admire Jim," she said, "but that's all. There'll never be anything between us." She saw his eyes light up and relief wash over his face, and she smiled at him. "Go back and help him. Then come to me. He'd help you if things were the other way around."

"I think maybe he would," Holly said thoughtfully. He sat still, silent for a few moments, then his face cleared. "I'll do it, Belle. Not just for you either," he added quickly, "but because it's the right thing to do. Meade's wrong in all this, and he's got to be stopped." He pulled the team up and jumped out, throwing the reins to Belle.

"Drive on right along this road, and you'll come into town near about morning. You'll be all right." He raised his voice and went on, "Mrs. Reynolds, I'm going back and give Jim a hand. We'll get word back to you as soon as we get this thing settled."

Dave untied his horse from the back of the wagon, swung into the saddle, and turned back along the road. Belle spoke to the horses, and they began a faster pace. Mona said, "That's strange. I didn't think Dave and Jim got along."

Lillian Reynolds answered, "They're both good men, and I'm glad to see that Dave's got that kind of spirit in him." She looked up at Belle, who was driving the team expertly, sitting quietly, her back ramrod straight, and went on in a low voice, "Out of all this something good might come."

Mona was less hopeful. "It's a war, Mother," she sighed. "I don't see how anything good can come out of it." She was worried and showed it. "I don't think Lew should have stayed. It would kill him if anything happened to his father."

"Sometimes I guess men come to a place like that, and maybe women, too. When they have to decide what's really important." She gave her daughter a knowing glance and went on, "I believe Lew thinks you're more important than anything else. Isn't that right?"

"I don't know," Mona said in a stricken voice. "I don't know what I think, Mother, it's all happening so fast." She was silent for a while, then said, "I'm so afraid something might happen to Lew. What does that mean?"

"It means that you have grown up, Mona," she said gently. They talked no more, and the three women sat quietly as the wagon made its way along the dark road toward Banning.

# SEVENTEEN
*Trapped!*

By the morning of the second day of dodging Slash A, the fugitives were ravenous. They had brought no food with them when they left Sun Ranch, and the strenuous labor of moving around to avoid the big crew that searched for them had taken its toll. Reno looked over the small group, estimating how much strength he could count on. There was Pack Ganton, who was tough enough, but only he, Ollie Dell, and Patch Meeks were left of the original crew. Easy Jones was a tough fighter, he knew. Then there was Lee, but Reno didn't want him to be thrown into the action. He was convinced that Holly was a man who could stand fast. And he had no doubts about the toughness of Lew Meade, though he was less certain about the young man's willingness to throw lead against his own family. He cast a look at Deacon Boone and somehow knew that the cook would not fail to do what had to be done. But Chris—Reno stared at the young man and was not at all sure. He's going to be a good man, he thought, but this is pretty tough going for a city boy. All of them were tired and on edge, and he knew that he couldn't hold the bunch together long without something to eat.

A rifle shot sounded faintly and far off to the east, and Easy turned toward it instantly. "They're moving closer," he observed. "We won't be able to stay here long, Jim."

"No," Reno agreed, "but I don't know which way to go. I don't know this country. We're liable to blunder around and walk right into them."

"I know it," Lew Meade spoke up. "I know this country. Tell me what you want to do, and I'll take you where you need to go." The others looked at Meade, and he flushed slightly for he knew what they were thinking. But he just raised his chin and stood a little firmer, saying nothing, and Reno was impressed with the young man.

"I don't know how many men they've got," Jim said slowly. "At least twenty, maybe more. We won't have a chance in a head-on shoot-out. We're gonna have to outsmart 'em."

Easy suddenly grinned at him and said, "Well, let's us just play like they're Yankees and we're Rebs, Jim. We spent most of our time durin' the war outsmartin' the Yankees, ain't that right?"

"These cowboys are smarter than those Yankees, I reckon," Jim said, smiling wearily. Then he sobered, nodding agreement. "But you're right, Easy, it's like the war. The Yankees always had bigger armies than we had, so it was people like Stonewall who knew how to march the legs off men and make a hundred seem like a thousand. Maybe we could pull off something like that."

Pack Ganton looked up sullenly. "I think it's crazy," he said. "Sooner or later they're gonna surround us. Some of those boys know this part of the world. And when they get here, we're dead meat."

"If you don't like it, pull out," Reno said harshly. "You've been looking for an excuse ever since things got tough."

Ganton flushed and stuck his chin out. "I'll stick. But after this dance is over, you can find yourself another boy, Mr. Reno."

The talk died down, and Jim walked around slowly, trying to collect his thoughts. The others said little. After a while he came back and said, "We have to make a move. So here's what we'll do."

He began to outline his plan, and when he was through, Ollie Dell laughed out loud. His face was scratched by the rough country they had come through, and he was sunburned and hungry, but was young and tough enough to snap back. "Lemme in on that little bunch, Jim!" he said gleefully. He looked over at Easy Jones and waved toward him. "I think me and Easy can handle it all right."

Easy nodded at Jim in agreement. "Why, shore, me'n this young feller'll bring them boys in. It'll be like my Uncle Seedy and the bear!"

Jim knew the men needed a moment of lightness, so he went for it with a slight smile. "What about your Uncle Seedy and the bear?"

"Waal," Easy said, a light in his blue eyes, "as I unnerstan' it, you fellers are gonna hole up somewheres, and me'n Ollie are gonna go stir up them fellers from Slash A. We're gonna try to make 'em think our whole bunch is there. And then when they come at us, we're gonna hightail it and run back to where you folks is waitin'. And then when they sashay in, it'll be just like they found them a hornet's nest. Is that the plan?"

"Yep. That's it," Jim said, amused. "What about your Uncle Seedy?"

"One time my Uncle Seedy and his nephew Josie went bear huntin'. They holed up in an old cabin there one night, and Josie was tellin' Seedy how that he, Josie, was the best bear skinner in the hills, that he could skin a bear clean 'fore a man could blink more'n a coupla times, but it didn't do no good since Seedy sure weren't much of a bear hunter and never was gonna find one to be skint. Shore enough, they had been plumb scarce.

"So the next morning Seedy had got enough of it. So he went out lookin' for a bear. And he hadn't got more than two hunnerd feet from the cabin when there rose up the biggest grizzly he ever seed in his whole life. Seedy throwed down on him and the chamber snapped. It was empty. Seedy throwed his gun down and made for the cabin, the bear right on his heels, lookin' as big as one of them dinosaurs I heared about. Well, the door, he'd left it open, and he made for it hard as he could."

Easy looked around to see if his audience was listening, which they all were, and then went on, "He got right there at that door, don't you see, and then the bear made a swatch at him, but Uncle Seedy, he jumped outta the way. So the bear, he just kept a-goin' and run right into the cabin, where Josie was. Uncle Seedy, he slammed the door to and run around to the winder, and he looked in and there was that bear in there, roarin' around and chasin' Josie, and Seedy, he hollered, 'Now there, Josie, I done brung you one bear. You get that 'un skint while I go scare up another one!'"

A laugh went up from most of the men, and it eased some of the tension. Deacon Boone said, "I sure would admire to meet your Uncle Seedy!" Easy grinned heartily, enjoying the attention, and said, "C'mon, Ollie, let's me and you go get these fellers a bear."

Jim called out as they left, "We'll be right here, in that

little canyon, Easy. You lead them right on through, and we'll take care of the rest."

Easy and Ollie left, and when they were out of range Ollie said, "We better have full loads in our rifles and six-guns, Easy. There's quite a bunch of them fellas." They loaded in the saddle, and as they rode on, Ollie gave Easy a sidelong look and asked about Reno. "What about him? You known him long?"

"Well, he's all sorts of a feller," Easy said. "I seen lotsa men, and I can tell you he's one you could trust to tote the key to the smokehouse."

Ollie looked back over his shoulder, then spurred his horse a little faster. "Well, he better be. When we bring them Slash A people in there, you ever stop to think me and you are gonna be right there in the trap with 'em? If Reno and the others don't shoot 'em off of our backs, we're goners."

"Well," Easy shrugged and said lightly, "they can't kill us but once, now, can they?"

★  ★  ★

Three hours had gone by and Jim had taken the men around, showing them where to take their positions. There was a natural canyon surrounded by walls of earth ten to twenty feet high and crowned with a great many trees. With an experienced eye, Jim had looked over the ground and moved each man around, saying, "When I give the signal, you get to this place. And when they ride in, it'll be Easy and Ollie right in front. Don't shoot them! Let them get inside! Don't shoot till you hear me fire. When you hear that shot, let go with everything you got."

After he had instructed all the men, there was nothing to do. Time wore on, and Chris finally came up to sit beside him.

"I hate to tell you this, Jim," he said reluctantly, "but my stomach's a little bit queasy. I've never been shot at before. And I sure never shot at anyone."

Jim Reno looked at him with understanding. "It comes to everybody," he said. "Don't worry about it, Chris. I remember the first battle of the war—Bull Run. Before the battle started my hands were shaking so I couldn't have loaded my gun if my life depended on it." Then he shrugged and went on, "But as soon as the battle starts, most of the time you don't have time to be scared." He looked at the boy with some regret. "But I wish you weren't here, Chris. This is not your kind of thing."

Chris looked at him resentfully. "It is now," he said stoutly. "It's my ranch, isn't it? If I won't fight for it, what kind of a man would I be?"

Reno continued to study him, letting a silence run on, then slapped him on the shoulder. "I sure wish Major Reynolds could be here. He'd be proud of you, Chris."

Chris flushed a little and sat straighter. "How long do you think it'll take?" Chris asked finally, after they had sat still for half an hour.

"Not too long. Did you hear those shots a while back?"

"No, I didn't hear anything."

"They were pretty far off. But there were one or two shots, and then a whole bunch of them. I think Ollie and Easy found them, took a couple of shots to get their attention, and then their whole bunch got together. Matter of fact, it's time to get the men into position." He stood up and called out, "All right! Get into position! And remember, no firing till you hear my shot!"

He looked down at Chris. "OK, Chris. Get behind that tree I showed you, and stay behind it while you shoot. Don't give up your cover for anything."

Reno took his position on the lip of the canyon at the foremost point, where he could see down through the line of trees where the trail led. He had to be sure that all the riders were in the trap before it was sprung.

He checked the loads in his rifle and his handgun, then leaned against a tree. Five minutes later he heard shots again, this time much closer. "They're getting closer!" he hollered. "Everybody stay under cover!"

Soon he picked up the sound of horses coming at a dead run and almost immediately saw Easy and Ollie lying low on their horses' necks and laying on the quirts. They ran into the canyon at full speed and Easy, who had spotted Jim with his hawk eyes, hollered, "Here's your bear! Now you kin get to skinnin'!"

They kept riding through the canyon, and within moments Jim saw a group of horsemen coming. They were strung out, dodging trees as they came through the timber, but when they reached the clearing they all bunched up together. He didn't see Simon Meade with them, and he was glad for that because he hadn't wanted to think about Lew shooting at his father. Bax LeFarge was in the front, and even as Jim threw a shell into the chamber he heard LeFarge yell, "Lester, you swing right when we get in there! Red, you take the left! I'll stay center!"

They charged in and scattered out, and Jim waited until the last man was through. He made a quick count—twenty-four riders. The front runners were firing at Ollie and Easy steadily. Even as he watched, Ollie and Easy came to a mound shaded by trees. Riding behind the trees they piled off their horses, whirled around, and began to fire at the oncoming riders. Jim glanced around, saw that the last man was in. He drew a bead on the man to the far left, pulled the trigger, and the man gave a cry and grabbed his shoulder. He didn't fall out of the saddle, but as Reno's gun went off, rifle fire began from all over.

Bax LeFarge tried to gather his men together, but he could see nobody to shoot at.

"They're up on the ledge!" Lester Box yelled wildly. "We're in a trap!"

Red DeQueen saw only one way out and hollered, "Bax! We gotta go back the way we came in! They got us ringed!" He turned to go, but as he spurred his horse a bullet knocked him out of the saddle, and he fell limply to the ground.

Panic set in on the Slash A men, and they fired wildly at the unseen marksmen up above them, but there were no targets they could really shoot at. Two more men fell, and more than a few were wounded.

"I'm gettin' outta here!" Box yelled. "They're gonna butcher us!"

He turned, driving his horse back through the opening. The rest stopped milling around aimlessly and turned to follow him. Shots followed them as they ran, and another man fell from the saddle. Immediately Reno came scrambling down the incline, saying, "Get mounted! We're going after them!"

There was a loud cheer from somebody, and soon they were on their horses, quickly pursuing the Slash A men. LeFarge, seeing the horses behind them, hollered, "Break up! Break up! We'll meet back at the ranch!" Half of the men veered off to the left, led by Lester Box, and the other half followed LeFarge. By the time Jim and his crew got there, he saw clearly what had happened.

"Look!" he said, pulling his horse up. "They split!"

"Why don't we split and go after them?" Chris said with

excitement. His face was pale for he had been one who knocked a man out of the saddle, but still his mouth was grim and determined.

"No, there would be too many for us, still," Reno said firmly. "Is anybody hurt?"

"Aw, I got me a scratch on my leg," Deacon said, "but it ain't much." He had joined in the fight despite continued protests from Reno that he ought to keep out of it, and now he asked, "What do we do next, Jim?"

Reno thought hard, then said, "We'll all take out after one of these bunches. I don't know who's leading which, but we'll either catch 'em or run 'em plumb out of the country. That'll leave us half the crew to fight when we take on Slash A."

"That sounds good to me," Dave Holly said, and they all spurred their horses to the left.

★ ★ ★

All of Banning knew exactly what was going on when the three women came into town as the sun rose. They went immediately to the sheriff's office, and Lige Benoit asked directly, "Trouble out at the ranch?" He listened quietly while Lillian Reynolds told him what had happened. When she finished he said tightly, "I hate to hear it, but it's been building up for a long time. You want me to send for a federal man, Mrs. Reynolds? I don't reckon he could do much, but he could stop this thing for a while."

Lillian Reynolds answered with spirit, "No. We'll fight this battle ourselves, Sheriff."

"If I can do anything, let me know. I wish that was my territory out there, but my authority ends with the city limits here. You know that, ma'am."

"Yes, I know, Sheriff. And I thank you for your interest."

As they left Lige, Mona said, "We have to get something to eat. There's nothing else we can do now. If we don't hear something by this afternoon, I'm going to get a horse and ride out there."

"I'll go with you," Belle said.

They went over to the hotel and started to enter the restaurant, but Belle said sharply, "Wait a minute!" and the other two women stopped behind her. Simon Meade was sitting at a table alone with a plate of food that he was toying with. He did not see the women, and he looked old and tired.

"You can wait here if you want or take a table. I'm going to talk to that man," Mona said in a determined voice.

Her mother looked at her in surprise and asked, "What are you going to say to him, Mona?"

Mona's face was fixed in a cast of anger. "You won't have to wonder. I'm going to say it loud enough for everyone to hear." She walked up to the table where Meade sat, and the big rancher looked up with surprise on his face as she planted herself square in front of him. He started to rise, but her voice caught him and held him still.

"Don't get up," Mona said coldly. "I'll not expect any manners from you, and you're not going to get any from me. Do you know who I am?"

"Why—you're the Reynolds girl."

"That's right, Ramona Reynolds. And I'm going to tell you exactly what kind of a man you are, Simon Meade!"

A flush came to Meade's face, and he said, "If you were a man, you wouldn't talk like that."

"If you were a man, you wouldn't be sending those killers of yours against women!" she retorted with scorn. "What makes you think you own the earth, Simon Meade? Do you think you have title to the whole planet?" She began to excoriate him, her voice loud and clear, and the other people in the restaurant made no pretense at eating but stared at the drama unfolding before them. They had seen Simon Meade walk roughshod over everyone in the valley, and now this small girl was ripping him to pieces with her voice.

Meade interrupted long enough to say, "Miss Reynolds, you don't understand how things are in this valley! There's only so much grass, and a man can have only so many cows, and what kind of a man would I be if I didn't make the best ranch that I could?"

"Are cows more important than a son, Mr. Meade?" Mona demanded.

The question seemed to strike Meade like a physical blow. He knew that the valley was talking about how his son had left him, walking away from his inheritance and all that Simon had built up for him. Now this girl was throwing it in his face. He winced painfully and muttered, "It's none of your business, girl!"

Mona saw that he was hurt by her words and said slowly and deliberately, "Do you know that your son is out there with our men? Trying to help us hang on to our ranch? And that he might be dead right now from one of your gang's bullets?"

Meade had not known, and her words at first seemed to have no meaning. Then his hands began to tremble, and he stood to his feet. "What—what are you talking about?"

"I am talking about your son," Mona said distinctly. "He's out there in the Short Hills, trying to stay alive, trying to save my family from your hired killers! One of our men is dead already, and by now, maybe more. And your son is right in the middle of it." She paused, staring at him with growing disdain. "I'm glad he's a better man than you are."

She turned to go, and Meade came around the table, following until he caught up to her. He took her arm and said, "Just a minute, miss. I didn't know any of this! I didn't know Lew was out there!"

"Would it have made any difference if you had known?" she snapped, her eyes flashing. "You've never understood Lew, and you never will. You're blind! You're so greedy, you'd throw your own son away for another dollar!"

Meade looked over and saw Lillian and Belle staring at him. He said, "Mrs. Reynolds, why did you send your crew over to raid my place? They rustled a hundred of my cattle! We followed their tracks right to your front door!"

Lillian Reynolds said with great dignity, "My men have never stolen one cow from you. If someone took those cattle, they were not from Sun Ranch."

There was no question of the truth and honesty in her voice, and suddenly a thought broke in Simon Meade's mind. *Jack Bronte! Bronte could have taken those cattle and led them over there to Sun to make me start a war with the Reynoldses.* The more he thought of it, the more certain he was, and sweat broke out on his face. He said, "Somebody did. That's the reason I brought the men over—to get an accounting."

Mona looked at him with contempt. "Well, you can stay here and go to the bank and count your money. But I'm going out to find out what's happening!"

Simon Meade had never been a man to explain himself and could not for the life of him come up with a reply to this fiery girl who stood so proudly before him. He brushed past them and strode out the door, his shoulders stooped. As he left, talk began to hum around the restaurant, and all eyes were fixed on the three women. Mona walked up to Belle and Lillian and said, "I'm sorry if I've upset you, Mother. But I had to tell that man what I thought of him. Now, let's get something to eat. And if they're not back by afternoon, I say let's go back and find them!"

They sat down and ordered and, though they had no appetite, forced themselves to eat. Belle said with her eyes fixed on Mona, "I always thought I had a temper! I thought you were going to shoot Meade!"

Mona blushed a little and said passionately, "He's so blind! He's got everything in the world! Money, a fine ranch, and a fine son! And he doesn't even know it."

Lillian said wistfully, "Some people are like that. They have everything, and they let life go by, and when they come to the end of it find that they haven't really found what was good. I feel sorry for him."

"Sorry for him!" Mona exclaimed. "I'd like to see him out there dodging bullets like Lew!"

Belle sipped her coffee, thinking about what Lillian had said. "I guess I would have felt that way once, Mona, but now I just feel like your mother. I'm sorry for Simon Meade. He's old, and now he's alone, no one to lean on. He's lost his son because even if Lew's all right, he'll never go back to Slash A, I don't think. So what does Simon Meade have?" She looked at Mona with compassion in her eyes, and the three women fell silent.

They finished their meal and soon left. The waitress said to the cook, "Boy, that Ramona Reynolds is a handful, ain't she? I thought she was gonna shoot ol' man Meade! She looked mad enough!"

"She sure did," the cook agreed. "Never did like to see a woman shoot a man in my restaurant. Makes people lose their appetite."

★　★　★

Bax LeFarge led his party up to the pocket where they were challenged almost at once by the lookout. Soon he was standing in front of Jack Bronte, pouring out his story.

Bronte listened carefully, his eyes veiled, and finally LeFarge said, "Get your bunch together. With what you got and what I got left, we can handle this. Let's go into town and get Reno and that bunch!"

Bronte looked over the shattered Slash A crew, three of them with slight wounds, all of them whipped. "That bunch is no good," he scowled, "and from what you tell me, Reno and the Sun people have probably caught up with your bunch by this time. You ain't got nothing left to fight with, Bax!"

Bax stared at Bronte vacantly. "You mean—you're pullin' out?"

"No, I mean I'm pullin' my horns in." Bronte smiled. He made a dangerous figure as he stood there, keeping his hand close to his gun. "You're washed up, LeFarge, and I would be too if I followed you down to that town. I didn't get to be as old as I am by stickin' my head in a noose. I'm gonna hide out in the pocket till the smoke clears. I'll still get what I want out of Slash A, but I'll pick my own time to do it. Now, if you take my advice you'll pile outta here and keep ridin' and get as far away from Slash A as you can."

One of the riders, who had been shot in the right forearm, looked up and said, "That's good advice, and I'm taking it." Four of the other men nodded, and Bax cursed them all roundly but saw that it was too late. He angrily threw himself on his horse and rode out, back toward Slash A. Bronte watched him go, then grinned at his lieutenant, saying, "Well, it was almost a good thing, but it's over now. We'll have to go back to gettin' rich the slow way, I guess. For now, that is." He stared at the disappearing trail of dust that LeFarge left and said, "I got a feelin' we won't be seein' Mr. LeFarge anymore. We sure won't if he goes up against Jim Reno."

# EIGHTEEN
## *Shoot-out!*

Simon Meade had made the trip from Banning to Slash A probably a thousand times, but never was the trip so long as the one he made after being verbally assaulted by Ramona Reynolds. He reached the ranch totally exhausted, practically fell off his horse, and wearily entered the ranch house.

Shorty Robbins, the cook, a short fat man with a mouthful of gold teeth, met him, saying, "You want something to eat, Mr. Meade?"

Meade shook his head without answering and went straight into his study. He sat down in the big chair behind his desk, almost collapsing. Robbins stuck his head in later to say, "They're not back yet, Mr. Meade. You reckon I oughta start cookin' dinner for 'em?"

Meade said abruptly, "No." Robbins pulled his head back and disappeared.

All that afternoon Meade sat at the desk, staring blindly at the papers in front of him. At about two o'clock he heard the sound of riders approaching. He blinked and passed his hand over his face, as one who awakens himself from sleep, then slowly lifted himself out of the chair and walked out onto the front porch.

Somehow he was not surprised to see Jim Reno, the young Reynolds boy, and others from Sun Ranch. He saw his own men, too, a few of them, eight or so, and said nothing as Reno dismounted and came over to speak to him.

Reno was tired, his face lined with fatigue. But there was an inner strength his weariness could not drown. His voice was sharp as he said, "Meade, we busted up your crew. Some of them won't be coming back. Two of them, I think, cashed in their chips. We opened the door, and they didn't have to come through," Reno said with regret. "It's a shame when a man has to die for a few dollars."

Meade looked past Reno, his eyes searching the riders. "Where's my son?" he asked, almost fearfully.

"I sent him on back to town. He's all right, if that's what you're wondering about." He watched for a sign on Meade's face and was surprised at how old and wan the man looked. Meade was sixty, but had been strong and in good health; now he looked ten years older. Lines had crept into his face, and his flesh was sagging around his jowls. His hands were not steady, and he looked smaller than before. Reno said almost gently, "It's all over, Meade. Your crew's scattered. I don't know where the rest of them are. I guess some of them will be drifting back. But I'm here to tell you," Reno continued, his voice becoming more harsh, "if you send one more rider against Sun, we'll be back and won't leave a building or a cow standing." Reno's voice was quiet and menacing as he looked at Meade without wavering. "Do you understand that?"

Meade stared at Reno and made no answer. He was empty and could not think of a reply. Finally he said, "I'll bring the men back and bury them here on the ranch, if you'll tell me where they are."

Reno softened a little and said, "I've got a man bringing them back." He started to say something else but saw that it would be useless. Moving back to his horse, he mounted and said, "Come on. Let's go."

The crew rode off, and one of the Slash A hands, Charlie Cole, tarried while the others straggled off toward the bunkhouse. "It was bad, Mr. Meade," he said quietly. Cole had been with Meade for years and had argued steadily against letting Bax LeFarge run roughshod over others in the valley. And now he brought that up. "LeFarge oughta be the one dead out there in that valley," he said bitterly. "He brought all this on. I don't know how he did it, but he had Jack Bronte in on it."

Meade looked at him and blinked his eyes as if trying to think. "You're the new foreman, Charlie," he said. "Pass the word around that any of the boys can stay that want to. There won't be any more raids. We'll just run the ranch we have."

Cole's face mirrored astonishment, then a pleased smile came over it. "Now you're showing sense, Mr. Meade! You got the best ranch I ever saw, and if we'll just tend to our business, it can be better yet." He turned and walked away rapidly to the bunkhouse, filled with new energy and anxious to assume his new duties.

Meade turned slowly and went back into the house. He washed his face in cool water and went in to try to eat. But he had no appetite. Finally he went in and lay down on the bed, boots and all, and dozed off wearily, his sleep troubled and restless.

He heard someone calling his name and snapped awake. Getting off the bed, he rubbed his face and walked out of the bedroom to find the cook, saying, "Bax wants to see you, boss. I put him in the study."

"Thanks, Shorty."

Meade walked to the study and found Bax LeFarge standing stiffly in front of his desk. "I guess you heard what happened, didn't you?" LeFarge snapped. His eyes were red-rimmed, and his lips made a white line as anger seemed to emanate from him and spill over, leaving an aura of tension in the room.

Meade took a deep breath and stepped closer to him. "I heard. Now we've got dead men, LeFarge—and I'm holding you responsible." He watched his words strike against LeFarge and continued relentlessly, "You and Bronte brought this on, didn't you? You had him move some of our cows over to Sun so I'd think they were raiding us. Don't bother to deny it," he said wearily. He walked over to his desk, opened the drawer, and took some bills out of a small tin box. Handing them to LeFarge, he said coldly, "Just get out of here. Get your gear, and don't come back!"

"You're firing me?" LeFarge was incredulous. He stared at Meade, then spat out, "You can't do that to me! I've put in eight years of work on this place!"

"I wish you had never set foot on it," Meade said, growing angry himself. "You're the one that kept saying we oughta run roughshod over people, and like a fool I listened to you! It's one thing to be tough—it's another thing to fire on women and children! Now get out of here, LeFarge!" For one moment Meade thought the burly rider would draw on him even though he was not armed. He waited a moment, then turned and stalked out of the room.

LeFarge cursed, kicked the desk, then left the house and

mounted up. Lester Box caught up with him and asked, "What happened?"

"The old man's running us off," he answered scornfully. "Me, anyway, and I guess that means you, too."

Box shrugged. "I don't care, Bax. Let's get out of here. We can find some new country, maybe try a little gold mining out at Virginia City."

Bax LeFarge cast a bitter glance at the ranch house, then turned to face Box. "All right. But we got one chore to do," he snarled between gritted teeth. "I ain't leavin' here till I settle with Jim Reno. If it hadn't been for him, things would have gone all right."

Box, who had not forgotten the way Reno had bested him first at the stage and now in this war, grinned wickedly. "I guess we got time for that. Between the two of us, we oughta be able to put him out pushin' up daisies."

The two wheeled their horses and headed out, leaving a trail of dust rising in the air as they went.

★  ★  ★

As the Sun crew rode into Banning the next morning at nine o'clock, Belle was standing at the window of the hotel, in the room she was sharing with Mona. "They're back!" she cried.

"Are they all there?" Mona asked, running to the window. The two women stared at the group and saw that the whole crew had returned.

"Come on!" Belle cried joyfully. "Let's go down!" She led the way, the two women almost running across the lobby and then breaking into a run on the street. The men were getting off their horses, and Belle stopped, waiting, her eyes fixed on Dave Holly.

Holly stepped out of the saddle, tossed his reins over the rail, then walked toward where Belle was waiting. He was searching her face, and he suddenly saw a welcome there that he had never seen before, and a streak of pure joy ran through him. When he got close, she held out her hands and he grasped them. She said breathlessly, "Oh, Dave, you're all right! Lew said you were OK, but I just couldn't believe it until I saw you!"

Holly held her hands, pressing them tightly. He wanted to kiss her right there in the street, but instead said only, "I'm all right." He stepped just a little closer and dropped his voice. "You know—it's good to know somebody cares. I've been alone a long time, Belle. I—I guess that's why I wrote that letter to you." He pulled her aside, and they began to walk together, oblivious of the others. As they went slowly down the street, he said, to get it off his chest, "I've got to say this now, Belle. I was wrong about you. Or wrong about me, I guess," he stumbled. "I ain't been no angel myself, Belle, but I think people have to start where they are." He was forming the words carefully, awkwardly. "There's no yesterdays, not for us. I love you now, and I always will. What went before—well, that's dead and buried."

Belle stopped walking and turned him around to study his face. She had always known he was an honest man, and he was easy to read. She was sure now, for the first time, that to him her past made no difference. She whispered quietly, "Yes, that's the way it is for us, isn't it, Dave?" She saw his desire to take her in his arms, and she shook her head, still speaking very softly. "Not now." Then a flash of merriment touched her eyes. "Later, we'll see."

Dave Holly grinned, fully and freely, and then a burst of

laughter bubbled out of his lips. He wanted to shout, to pull his gun and fire shots in the air. She saw the release of spirit in him and said primly, "Save some of that excitement until later, please. I'll expect a little more courting than I've had up until now." She turned around, and they walked back to where the others were talking.

Jim had gone at once to Lillian and said to her, "I think we're all right, Lillian. Meade's given up, and most of his crew—the rough ones at least—are running for cover. I believe it's going to be all right."

Lillian smiled at Jim, then turned to look at Lew Meade, who had just joined the group, and Mona and Chris, who were standing, watching Reno. She said, "I hope so, Jim. If it does work out, we'll know who to thank."

Reno was embarrassed and pretended not to hear Lillian. "And we've got work to do. I've got to go talk to the sheriff about the loss of Wilson. Some of the rest are shot up a little, but not much. Let's get them taken care of, then we can celebrate."

It was no more than an hour later when most of the chores Reno had mentioned were taken care of. They had gone to the sheriff's office to explain some of the details of the raid, and Lige Benoit listened carefully, but his mind seemed to be on other things. He knew he had no authority in the matter, and he knew that no federal man would come. As Reno was delineating the story of the raid, he suddenly looked out the window, then his eyes darted to Lew Meade, who was in the office with Reno and the Reynolds family. "There's your dad, Lew," he said quietly.

Lew Meade straightened up, and his face grew tense. He turned and walked out onto the porch, the others following.

Simon Meade saw them and guided his horse over in front of the office, dismounted slowly, almost painfully, and tied the animal to the hitching post. He came up to the group, stood in front of Lillian Reynolds, and pulled off his hat. His hair was very white in the sunshine, and he made a pathetic shape as he stood there, his face deeply troubled.

He lifted his eyes and gazed on his son, but something he saw in Lew's face made him tighten his lips, and he turned back to Lillian. "Mrs. Reynolds," he said thickly, "I've come to tell you that you'll have no more trouble from Slash A." He hesitated, then said something he had not said for years. "I'm sorry."

He looked back at Lew and at the girl beside him, the girl that had so raked him with her words that he still felt almost raw, and waited, hoping that one of them would speak. Neither of them did. Slowly he turned, put his hat on, and walked away.

"Come on back in the office," Sheriff Benoit said, "and I'll get all this down."

The others went in, but Reno pulled at Lew's arm and held him there, and Mona stayed beside him. They both looked at him expectantly, waiting to hear what he would say, but Reno stood silently. He was a smaller man than Lew Meade, the other towering over him, but yet he was solid and thick, and there was a look on his face that held their attention. They had both seen him go through things that would have felled a lesser man, and now Lew's voice sounded respectful. "What is it, Jim?"

Reno pulled off his hat, stared at it, rolled it around in his hands, then replaced it. "You know, Lew, your dad's been wrong, but that's common to all of us." He looked up, locking his sharp gaze with that of the tall young cowboy, and continued, "Some of the fellas that fell beside me when I was in the war, after they fell all I could think of was what I could have done for them." His voice dropped even lower and he said, almost in a whisper, "You can't make things up to a dead man, Lew. You can only show something good to the living."

Lew blinked, and he felt Mona's hand tighten on his arm. He waited for Reno to go on, but Jim stood there, seemingly oblivious of the wondering looks on the faces of the two in front of him. Mona was feeling a compunction, for although she had been filled with rage at Lew's father she knew now that her future lay with this tall young man beside her. She had some idea, also, of what hating did to a person, and she was afraid she had set off a chain reaction that would rise up to trouble them in days to come.

"Maybe Jim's right," she said hesitantly. "Why don't—"

At that moment a man stepped out from behind the bank, which was seventy yards down the street, and caught her eye. She gave a little gasp and said, "Jim! Look!"

He whirled around almost before she had finished the words and saw Bax LeFarge stepping out into the street, looking directly at him. "Get her out of here, Lew," Reno snapped.

He turned and walked toward LeFarge, his mind running rapidly. He was aware that suddenly someone was beside him and knew it was Lew. He glanced to see that Mona had gone back up the steps and was standing beside Benoit, who had stepped out with Chris and Lillian. Other people had suddenly moved off the street, noticing the stance of LeFarge, knowing it spelled trouble.

"Better get off the street, Lew," Jim said. "No sense in you getting mixed up with this."

"I don't see it like that," Lew said calmly. He did not break his stride and only when LeFarge stopped twenty yards away did Reno halt, and Lew dropped slightly behind him.

"I've been looking for you, Reno," LeFarge said. His eyes were muddy with rage, and he kept his hand close to his gun butt. "You think you're top man, but not to me you ain't! I never saw the man I'd take water from, and I'm gonna give you a chance to go for your gun first—then I'll kill you."

As always, when action was imminent, time seemed to slow down for Jim Reno. The streets and people faded until the only thing he saw clearly was Bax LeFarge, who stood there, a huge ugly shape, ready to kill.

"Clear out, Bax," Jim said evenly. "It's all over. You've nothing to gain by a shoot-out."

LeFarge laughed viciously. "I knowed you was yellow! You may be handy with your fists, but I'm tellin' you you're finished, Reno."

Reno was aware that LeFarge would not back down, and a great regret swept over him. He said mildly, "I wish you'd left, Bax."

"You knew I wouldn't, didn't you? I'd never walk away from a fight. When I leave here, you won't be goin' anywhere."

Reno had his entire attention fixed on LeFarge, staring into his hate-filled eyes. His own nerves were straining, and at the first sign of a movement of LeFarge's right hand, he would go for his own gun.

Over on the sidewalk, Simon Meade had been caught by the sudden drama that was unfolding on the main street of Banning. The two men, Jim and Simon's son, Lew, were even with him, no more than ten feet away, but neither of them was watching him. Meade wanted to go and pull Lew away, but he knew the boy would not listen. Helplessly he stood there. Suddenly he saw the flash of a bright reflection on the second story over the bank. He squinted his eyes and made out the tip of a rifle that slowly slid out along the window ledge, trained directly on the two men in the street.

*A trap! An ambush!* his mind screamed. With a hoarse cry he threw himself toward the street. "Look out, Lew!" he yelled. Lew, whose nerves were also taut, turned in confusion. As the huge bulk of his father's body swung in front of him, a shot rang out. The force of the bullet drove Simon Meade into Lew, who staggered backward under his father's falling body.

"Jim!" Lew yelled, trying to free his gun, but his father's weight fell on him, and he tripped. The two men rolled in the dirt.

The sound of the shot caught Reno unprepared, for his entire focus had been on LeFarge. But the sudden explosion and the appearance of Simon Meade shook him. He saw the man fall and knew instantly that he had been shot by someone in hiding. When he whirled his head back, he saw that LeFarge had taken advantage of his break to go for his gun. LeFarge's .44 was half out of the holster before Jim even reacted. His hand made a stab, and by the time he had cleared leather, LeFarge got off a quick shot, and he felt the kiss of the bullet as it hissed past his ear.

He shot at LeFarge, saw it strike the man, turn him around, and drop him in the dust. Then, looking for the other man, he caught the reflection of the rifle above LeFarge, and in a split second lifted his gun and shot at the rifle sticking out of the window. A wild cry echoed in the street, and the rifle fell outside the window, clattering as it struck the sidewalk.

Benoit, running with his gun pulled, was watching the upper window. He called out without slowing down, "I'll go see who that was, Jim! Look out for LeFarge!"

As Benoit plunged into a side door of the bank, Jim walked over to where LeFarge was squirming in the dust. He had been hit in the side and was holding onto the wound with one hand but still had his gun in the other. His eyes looked up balefully, then filled with fear as Reno stood over him. He threw the gun down, gasping, "No more! I'm through, Reno."

Reno kicked the gun away and bent beside the man, looking at the wound. It looked bad, but he said to LeFarge, "I've seen men get over worse, LeFarge." Men were beginning to run toward them, and he told someone, "Get this one to the doctor." Then he turned and ran back to where Lew was kneeling beside his father. He dropped to one knee beside Mona, who had rushed out to Lew. "How is he?" Reno demanded.

Lew merely shook his head. He had pulled his father into a sitting position and looked at the blood that had come off on his hand. "He took a slug in the back," he whispered, "that was meant for me." His face was pale, and Reno saw that Mona was speechless with fright and shock.

At that moment Simon Meade's eyes fluttered open. He looked up, blinking in the bright sun. Then he recognized who it was that held him. He stared at Lew almost unbelievingly and said very plainly, "Lew . . . I was afraid—"

Lew waited for him to complete the sentence, and when his father coughed once and pain racked his face he said gently, "Don't try to talk, Dad. We'll get you to a doctor."

"Wait," Meade said faintly, "may not . . . make it." There was a huskiness in his voice, and he whispered urgently, "Ranch is yours . . . you'll do better . . . than I did." He stopped and then suddenly, in a gesture he had not made for years, reached up and touched the face of his son and whispered so faintly that Lew had to lean forward to catch it. "You're like . . . your mother."

"Come on," Reno urged, "let's get him to the doctor."

There was plenty of help to carry the big man to the doctor's office, where Doc Hardy had rushed after hearing the commotion. "Get his shirt off," he said quickly, "and let me take a look. Everybody clear out. Can't work with this mob around."

They all left the office, and when they got outside, Lige Benoit emerged from the door beside the bank. He came over and stood in front of Reno and said succinctly, "Lester Box. Drilled through the heart." He looked around at the men who were pulling LeFarge up to carry him to the doctor's office, but ignored that and said, "How's your dad, Lew?"

"Don't know." Lew's face was pale. "I never expected him to do anything like that."

Reno said quietly, "I guess we never know what we are until we see something we love threatened."

His words caused Lew's head to swivel around sharply, and he studied Reno, then nodded. He turned to Mona and said, "Come on. I'm going in there, I don't care what that doctor says."

The two of them disappeared, and Jim watched as they carried LeFarge in to wait his turn. He stood quietly in the street, glanced up at the window where Box had been, and regret slowly came over his face. Easy came over to stand beside him and knew what was going on in Reno's mind. "Well, he had his chance to walk away from it, James," he said staunchly. "You can't fault yourself for what you done."

"I guess not," Reno said sparsely, then seemed to shake himself. "Where's Lee?"

"There he is over there," Easy said. "I b'lieve he woulda been fillin' LeFarge full of lead hisself if I hadn't been there to stop him."

Reno walked over to Lee, and Easy followed. The three of them spent the next half hour waiting for the doctor to come out. He did not, but when Lew Meade walked out with Mona close beside him, one look at his face told them the story.

"Bullet missed the lung," Lew said, taking a deep breath. "He'll need some good nursing for a while."

Mona reached up and touched his arm. "I've had some practice, Lew. You think I'll do?"

The two turned aside, and as they left, Reno smiled and said to Easy and Lee, "Looks like things are gonna work out."

"Not with Bronte up in the hills," Easy warned. "He'll be comin' down sooner or later, and he'll be a-givin' trouble not just to Sun, but to Slash A, too, now that Meade's whittled down to size."

Reno stood, watching Dave Holly and Belle as they walked along, deep in conversation. A thought came to him, and a smile touched his lips. Then he turned to answer Easy's observations. "There's always a Bronte of some kind up in the hills, Easy. Just gotta learn to take 'em one at a time."

Lillian then approached Reno, accompanied by Chris. They walked up, and Lillian said, "Jim, I hate to ask you to stay, but could you, just for a little while, to help us? I know Jack Bronte won't leave us alone for long. I don't think we can survive without you."

Reno grinned at Chris, saying, "Well, this young fella here's going to be running things pretty soon. But just for a while, we'll stay."

As Lillian and Chris walked away, Easy said, "Ain't never

satisfied 'less you're hip-deep in somebody's troubles, are you, James? Just born to be a natural do-gooder! Here I was ready to go taste the fleshpots of the big city, and now we're gonna be nursin' them blasted cows again!"

Reno looked at him, and the pressure was suddenly gone. He threw his head back and laughed, reached over and grabbed Lee by the back of the neck and gave him a shake. "Come on, you little fire-eater! Let's go get something to eat!"

The three of them moved down the street, and Easy began telling of how he had once won a pancake-eating contest in Butte, Montana. . . .

# In addition to this series . . .

## RENO WESTERN SAGA
#1 Reno   0-8423-1058-4
#2 Rimrock   0-8423-1059-2
#3 Ride the Wild River   0-8423-5795-5
#4 Boomtown   0-8423-7789-1

. . . look for more captivating historical fiction from Gilbert Morris!

## THE WAKEFIELD DYNASTY
This sweeping saga follows the lives of two English families from the time of Henry VIII through four centuries of English history.
#1 The Sword of Truth   0-8423-6228-2
#2 The Winds of God   0-8423-7953-3
#3 The Shield of Honor (New! Spring 1995)   0-8423-5930-3

## THE APPOMATTOX SAGA
Intriguing, realistic stories capture the emotional and spiritual strife of the tragic Civil War era.
#1 A Covenant of Love   0-8423-5497-2
#2 Gate of His Enemies   0-8423-1069-X
#3 Where Honor Dwells   0-8423-6799-X
#4 Land of the Shadow   0-8423-5742-4
#5 Out of the Whirlwind   0-8423-1658-2
#6 The Shadow of His Wings   0-8423-5987-7
#7 Wall of Fire (New! Spring 1995)   0-8423-8126-0

## Just for kids

## THE OZARK ADVENTURES
Barney Buck and his brothers learn about spiritual values and faith in God through outrageous capers in the back hills of the Ozarks.
#1 The Bucks of Goober Holler   0-8423-4392-X
#2 The Rustlers of Panther Gap   0-8423-4393-8
#3 The Phantom of the Circus   0-8423-5097-7

Gilbert Morris is the author of many best-selling books, including the popular House of Winslow series, the Reno Western Saga, and The Wakefield Dynasty.

He spent ten years as a pastor before becoming professor of English at Ouachita Baptist University in Arkansas and earning a Ph.D. at the University of Arkansas. Morris has had more than twenty-five scholarly articles and two hundred poems published. Currently he is writing full-time.

His family includes three grown children, and he and his wife, Johnnie, live in Orange Beach, Alabama.